Imprint of the Hand

More Legends and Stories of the Finger Lakes Region

The Heart of New York State

By Emerson Klees
Illustrated by Dru Wheelin

Friends of the Finger Lakes Publishing, Rochester, New York

For information, write:
Friends of the Finger Lakes Publishing
P. O. Box 18131
Rochester, New York 14618

Library of Congress Catalog Card Number 96-84782
ISBN 0-9635990-7-0

Printed in the United States of America
9 8 7 6 5 4 3 2 1

Cover design by Seneca Mist Graphics, Ithaca, New York
Book design by Dru Wheelin

Preface

MORE LEGENDS AND STORIES OF THE FINGER LAKES REGION: *The Heart of New York State* is a collection of Indian legends and of stories from within and around the Finger Lakes Region. It is a sequel to *LEGENDS AND STORIES OF THE FINGER LAKES REGION: The Heart of New York State*. The Heart of New York is bounded by the I-390 Expressway in the west, the New York State Thruway in the north, the I-81 Expressway and Route 13 in the east, and Route 17, the Southern Tier Expressway, in the south. The scenic Finger Lakes Region contains 264 municipalities in fourteen counties spread over 6,125 square miles.

This book contains twenty-one legends—three legends on each of seven topics:

 Lake Legends
 Evil Legends
 General Legends
 Ethereal Legends
 Native Origin Legends
 Destiny Legends
 Self-sacrifice Legends

It also contains sixty stories about the area—narratives of:

 Serpents / Strange Tales
 Travails / Tragedies
 Ordinary Stories / Observations
 Reminiscences / Rivalries
 Inventions / Ideas
 Eclectic / Extraordinary Stories
 Sources / Sites

This book contains some material reprinted from *PERSONS, PLACES, AND THINGS IN THE FINGER LAKES REGION; PERSONS, PLACES, AND THINGS AROUND THE FINGER LAKES REGION;* and *PEOPLE OF THE FINGER LAKES REGION*.

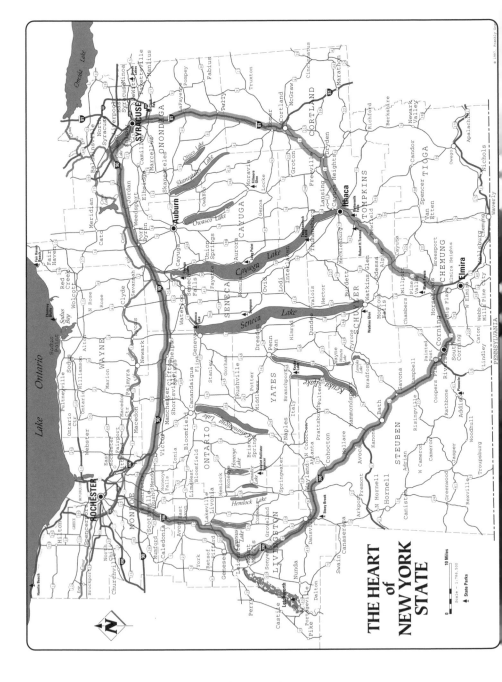

THE HEART
of
NEW YORK
STATE

iv

Table of Contents

Table of Contents

Prologue

 ### The Matriarchal Society of the Iroquois

he Iroquois established in their constitution of the Ho-de-no-sau-ne, the Confederacy of the Long House, that women's rights would always be protected by their laws. Iroquois boys and girls were the sons and daughters of the mother's clan; they were not the inheritors of the clan rights of the father. If a Seneca woman of the Bear Clan married a Mohawk, her children and their children would be Senecas of the Bear Clan down through the generations. This tribal law maintained the purity of clan descent.

The Iroquois mother was responsible for the care of her children during their infancy and childhood and was responsible for the development of their character. The father had no control or authority over his children until his sons matured and became his companions in the hunt and on the warpath.

Iroquois women owned property and continued to own it after they married. They could dispose of the property as they chose. By the Iroquois law of descent, children could not inherit property from their father, because they were not of their father's clan. They were inheritors of their mother's clan.

Women arranged all marriages for their children. A woman might consult with the elders of the clan, but the responsibility was hers. Settlement of all family disputes was the responsibility of the mother, with the advice of other clan members. If her child's marriage got into difficulty, the mother decided whether the couple should separate. Separations occurred rarely because they were considered a disgrace. If reconciliation was not possible, usually because of incompatibility, a divorce was granted. The divorced wife returned to the lodge of her mother with her children and her property.

When a chief died, a council was called to elect a new chief. The mother of the family in which the death occurred selected the most reliable male of her own line of descent as chief. She might consult with others, but the final decision was her responsibility. If the elected chief was derelict in his duties or did not measure up to expectations, the mother was responsible for removing him as chief and selecting another male in her line of descent to replace him.

Iroquois women were appointed to serve in religious feasts with men. Women were also responsible for all burial or death feasts. They were considered to be the guardians of all plants, particularly the "three sisters": beans, corn, and squash. Women were also the guardians of the "Chief" wampum belts that were sent to them by the great councils when a chief was elected. These wampum belts confirmed a nomination of a chief and were recognized as making the election of the chief legal.

Iroquois women had these rights long before pioneer settlers moved into the Finger Lakes Region. The first Women's Rights Convention was held in Seneca Falls on July 19-20, 1848, to address conditions that are difficult to envision today: women were not permitted to vote, to obtain a college education, or to own property, and their wages were turned over to their husbands. In cases of separation and divorce, guardianship was always given to the husband. By law, a woman's inheritance went to her husband. She was not entitled to the rights given automatically to men of the lowest station, whether they were born in the United States or were immigrants.

Native American women had a higher position in society and rights superior to those of the mothers, wives, and daughters of the white settlers of the region. However, the Native Americans were considered "uncivilized" by pioneer settlers who considered themselves "civilized."

Life in the Longhouse

he Iroquois lived in a world of luxuriant forests, beautiful lakes, rippling streams, rich soil, and plentiful fish and game. The patterns of their existence were fixed by the sun, rain, snow, and wind. Their life, which revolved around the seasons, was a challenge for survival against elements and enemies.

Early longhouses had the appearance of long, narrow wigwams with semi-circular roofs, that is, shaped like a barrel cut in half lengthwise. Their frames were made from two long rows of saplings placed ten feet apart. The tops of the saplings were bent over toward the other row and covered. Longhouses evolved with higher walls and a more rectangular shape. Eventually, peaked roofs were added.

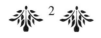

Most villages overlooked rivers and lakes and were situated on hills for reasons of defense and drainage. The Iroquois built sizable villages with palisades for protection against attack. They usually located their gardens on lower ground below the village. The women and children cultivated corn, beans, and squash in the village garden. Well-tended orchards grew within a short distance from the longhouses.

The Iroquois moved their villages every ten to twelve years. By that time, they had to travel farther for firewood, and the soil, without fertilization or crop rotation, had become less fertile. It was time to move on. The men chose the new site, cleared it of brush and trees, built new longhouses, and tilled the soil to prepare the garden for planting. Then, if they lived on a river, all of the family possessions were carried upstream in bark canoes.

Many people, who were members of multiple families, lived in one longhouse. A village was divided into clans, such as the bear, beaver, deer, eel, heron, snipe, turtle, and wolf clans. Members of the bear clan of a Mohawk tribe were relatives of bear clan members of an Oneida tribe. The Cayuga, Onondaga, and Seneca Nations each had nine clans, and the Mohawks and Oneidas had three each. Clan members did not intermarry.

Rows of bunk beds lined the inside walls of the longhouse. Each family unit had a twelve-foot section of the longhouse with bark interior partitions for privacy. Each family also had a fire pit with an overhead hole in the roof to allow smoke to escape. Longhouses were dark; the only light entered through doorways or smoke holes. Babies were kept in cradle boards or papooses until they were about two years old; then they toddled around the longhouse.

The change of seasons was important to the Iroquois. They viewed winter as a time to renew the body and the mind. They held mid-winter celebrations in January and February to welcome in the New Year and participated in dances and competitive games. False face society members, who wore masks representing healing spirits, danced around the longhouse fire and spread ashes around those who were ill to drive away evil spirits. Members of the corn husk society, who wore masks made from corn husks, also participated in the midwinter celebrations to thank the spirits of the harvest.

Snow Snake was one of the winter games played by the Iroquois. They crafted snakes from flexible pieces of wood over six feet long. Two eight-player teams alternated in tossing the snakes across a track of ice from which the snow had been brushed. Points were awarded based on the distance the snow snakes traveled over the ice.

In early March, Iroquois women moved the fire outdoors, and the men worked outside on warm days making and repairing nets to be used for fishing. Early spring was also the time for collecting and boiling maple sap to make maple sugar and syrup.

Tree bark was gathered in the springtime to make and repair lodge coverings and canoes. The Iroquois made a cut at the base and another about six feet up the trunk of birch, elm, hickory, and oak trees to peel off the bark after joining the two circular cuts with a vertical cut. They used a wooden wedge to gently separate the bark from the tree. Twine was made from the inner bark of selected trees.

Springtime was above all the time for planting seeds for the year's crop. Women did the planting, weeding, and harvesting of the major crops of beans, corn and and squash. Each clan cultivated their own plot, as directed by the clan mothers. They planted their seeds when the leaf of the oak tree was the size of a mouse's ear. The seeds were blessed, soaked in water for several days, and planted in mounded hills about five feet apart. The women also grew gourds to fashion into bowls, cups, and dippers for the water supply.

During the summer, the women and children gathered wild food, such as berries and roots. The men fished, fought, and worked around the longhouse. In early June, strawberry festivals were held in honor of the first fruit to ripen. The Iroquois considered strawberries sacred, believing that they lined the path to the Great Spirit. The Green Corn Ceremony was held in mid-August to thank the corn spirits for an abundant harvest and to invite them to return during the following growing season. Games such as lacrosse were played during the summer, and ash-splint baskets and clay pots were made during the warm months.

In the autumn, the men hunted and trapped, and the women harvested and preserved vegetables. The women dried corncobs on wooden boards, which allowed air to circulate around them. Then they scraped kernels off the cobs and stored the corn in bark-lined pits in the ground below the frost line. The corn was thus preserved and protected from scavenging animals. The women also dried beans and squash, which was cut into thin strips and draped from long lines to dry. Also in the fall, the women and children gathered acorns, beechnuts, butternuts, chestnuts, hazelnuts, and hickory nuts to make flour.

Braves used deadfalls, snares, and tomahawks to kill small animals. Deadfalls were heavy logs or stones that fell and crushed the animal when a trip was sprung. Before they received guns from the European settlers, they used bows and arrows to kill large animals, such as bear, deer, and elk. Squaws made breechcloths, dresses, leggings, pants, robes, shirts, and skirts from doeskin because it was lightweight and supple.

The Iroquois knew how to use the products of the wild to their advantage and how to survive the harsh northern winters. Until the

Revolutionary War, when many of their crops, orchards, and villages were destroyed by General Sullivan's expedition to central New York, the Iroquois Confederation was one of the most advanced Indian cultures on the North American continent.

 ## The Sullivan Campaign

n 1778, white settlers were massacred by Indians in Wyoming (Wilkes-Barre), Pennsylvania, and Cherry Valley, New York, causing considerable anxiety among the whites in the region. The British tried to convince their Indian allies, four of the six nations of the Iroquois Confederacy, to attack General Washington's Colonial Army from the west. On February 27, 1779, Congress authorized General Washington to form an expedition to remove this threat from the Iroquois.

Washington offered the command of the expedition to thirty-nine-year-old Major General John Sullivan, who had distinguished himself in the battles of Brandywine, Germantown, Trenton, and Princeton, and particularly in leading the bayonet charge at Butt's Hill. Sullivan's army assembled at Easton, Pennsylvania, stopped at Wyoming, Pennsylvania, to correct some supply problems and marched on to Tioga Point, now Athens, Pennsylvania.

Another element of the expedition started from Schenectady, commanded by Brigidier General James Clinton, Sullivan's second-in-command. They built 212 boats and moved up the Mohawk River to Canajoharie, where they carried the boats overland to Otsego Lake. They built a dam at Cooperstown, raised the level of Otsego Lake by two feet, and proceeded south to meet Sullivan at Tioga Point. Sullivan's men built Fort Sullivan at Tioga Point and waited for Clinton's forces to arrive.

Clinton arrived in late August, and both elements of the expedition marched on to Newtown, five miles south of Elmira. They were met there by a force of 1,000 to 1,500 men, comprised of Tories, Canadian Rangers, and Indians. The force opposing Sullivan was commanded by the Mohawk chief, Joseph Brant, who had been educated by Eleazar Wheelock, founder of Dartmouth College. Sullivan's army of over 3,000 routed Brant's force, partly because some of the Colonials worked in behind Brant's men, waiting in ambush. This was the only staged battle of the campaign. The expedition's next encampment was at Horseheads, where on the return journey, Sullivan's men shot thirty to forty worn-out pack horses. Later, the Indians lined the sun-bleached horse skulls along the trail, giving the town of Horseheads its name.

Sullivan's expedition moved through the Finger Lakes Region causing considerable destruction, particularly around Cayuga and Seneca Lakes. Of the six major lakes, Keuka Lake was the only one not visited by Sullivan's men. The army reached as far west as the Genesee River; they marched by the northern ends of Canandaigua, Honeoye, and Hemlock Lakes and the southern end of Conesus Lake. Sullivan sent a detachment to Conesus Lake to scout the Indian settlement at Genesee Castle. Fifteen of the twenty-four men in the scouting party were killed; Lieutenant Thomas Boyd and Sergeant Michael Parker were tortured, mutilated, and killed. Sullivan's men found their bodies at Genesee Castle, a settlement of 128 houses between Cuylerville and the west bank of the Genesee River.

On the expedition's return through the region, Colonel Peter Gansevoort was sent to Albany with a detachment of 100 men, who passed through the sites of Auburn and Skaneateles. At the close of the expedition, Sullivan reported that he had destroyed forty Indian villages, 160,000 bushels of corn, large quantities of other crops, and many acres of orchards.

Sullivan had complied with Washington's order: "It is proposed to carry the war into the heart of the country of the Six Nations, to cut off their settlements, destroy their next year's crops ... lay waste all the settlements around, so that the country may not only be overrun but destroyed." General Sullivan had accomplished the goals of removing the British threat from the west and of stopping the Six Nations from making war as a confederation. Unfortunately, he had also destroyed one of the most advanced Native American cultures that existed up to that time.

Chapter 1

Lake Legends

The Legend of Lake Eldridge

The Iroquois village of Shinedowa stood on the site of present-day Elmira. The village was surrounded by cornfields, plum trees, and apple orchards. Unusually shaped mounds that had been formed by flood waters were located south of the village along the Chemung River. Beyond these mounds were evergreen trees that hid the village's burial grounds. The mounds and the evergreens were the gates to the happy hunting ground. The squaws of the the tribe went there to weep for their dead relatives and friends.

Mt. Zoar dominated the surrounding hills. The council house was located in the center of the plain. The squaws sat on the ground around the council house when braiding rushes into multi-colored mats, making moccasins, and weaving baskets. As they worked, they passed the time of day and traded news. The chief's wife observed that her son, Owenah, had the evil eye. The Chief had gone to Seneca a moon ago, and upon his return she knew that he planned to convene the council to discuss the spell that had been cast over their son.

Another squaw replied that even the children could tell that there was something wrong with the chief's son. A third woman noted that the girls of the village avoided Owenah because his strange behavior scared them. This third squaw thought that her friend's son was definitely under an evil spell. The chief's wife reminded her friends that Owenah was always reserved, shy, and a little strange, but that they hoped that he would settle down and become a great chief like his father. However, for the last six months, he had done nothing to prepare himself to become a warrior or to hunt for the tribe.

One of the squaws said that:

Once no young brave could cope with Owenah in the hunt, and he was known in the lodges from Seneca to Tioga as among the bravest. But he has changed. He sits as idle as the painted leaves. He listens no more to the stories of war. His bow and arrows are neglected. He sharpens not his knife and he goes no longer to the lodge of the arrow maker for arrows. The younger braves look upon him with distrust, and the girls laugh at him or look at him askance, but he does not mind it. The old warriors have noticed his strange ways and say he will never be a warrior unless he rouses from his slumber.

Most of the tribe agreed with the observation that the evil eye was upon him.

Every day Owenah went into the swamps surrounding the bottomless lake. He took no weapons with him and he returned empty-handed with a distant look in his eye. The pride of the tribe had changed, and he was now a disappointment to his community. The village had hoped that Owenah would take over for the chief when his father became too infirm to lead. However, over the last few months he had become reserved and quiet, had avoided his friends, and had given up the hunt.

Every day he walked alone north toward the swamp surrounding the lake that the tribe called Ouwela. When his companions asked him to join the chase for wild game, he gave them vague excuses. He returned at the end of the day with no fish, game, or edible roots. When asked what he had done all day, he avoided the question. The rest of the tribe stayed away from the swamp because they considered it evil. In the past, many braves had been lured to the swamp by voices that called them and fires that attracted them. They were never heard from again. The green Piasau, or bird of doom, was known to go there; its eerie cry on dark nights had spread terror through the village.

Several years earlier a band of hunters from the village forced their way through the thicket to the shores of the lake, where one of the bravest of their numbers was seized by a terrifying monster that came up from the depths. The brave was pulled down into the lake and was never seen again. The rest of the party escaped, but they heard the cry of the Piasau as they made their way back to the village. They were terrified of this cry because they knew that the bird of doom could carry away a man with the ease that an eagle carried a fish.

The men of the tribe had sunk hundreds of feet of line into the lake and had found no bottom. The geese did not rest on the dark surface of the lake either on their migration south or on their return in the spring. No one but Owenah visited the bottomless body of water. The rest of the tribe wondered what interest he could possibly have in the lake. They didn't know that he had wandered into the swamp unintentionally about a year previously. He had stumbled upon a beautiful girl sitting on a fallen tree while arranging a wreath of wild flowers. He had never seen such breathtaking beauty.

She was slender and dressed like the girls of his tribe, but the many ornaments on her dress indicated that she was a princess. She was fairer than the girls in his village, and her eyes had a tender gleam in them. Her black hair fell well below her shoulders. Owenah was captivated by her and could think of nothing to say. She asked him why his arrows had found no game. He responded that his companions were hunting on the other side of the hill, and he decided to see if he could find game on this side of the hill.

She pointed and said, "If Owenah will go to that tall pine in the distance, he will find game." He was so surprised to hear his name pronounced by a stranger and in such a sorrowful tone that he was filled with wonder. He turned in the direction that she had pointed; by the time that he turned back toward her, she had disappeared. He had heard no noise, and he could not tell in which direction she had fled. He was filled with awe. As he walked in the direction of the tall pine, he heard the call of the Kalewee, the bird of evil omen. However, he could think of nothing but his beautiful companion. He saw nothing but her endearing image.

At the foot of the tall pine tree, Oweneh saw a white deer, which he killed with a single arrow. He hauled the deer back to the village and placed it at his mother's feet. She told him that she feared that evil would happen to him, because he had killed a white doe. She suggested that he tell no one about it.

Owenah could not get the beautiful girl by the lake out of his

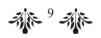

mind. He thought about her all the time; he was smitten. He returned many times to the fallen tree where he had seen her, but he always returned home disappointed. Winter came and went, and he didn't find her by the lake. One spring day he found her where he had seen her before. Again, she was arranging a garland of blossoms. She asked him why a hunter would come to the lake with its surrounding swamp, because there were neither fish nor game there.

Owenah hesitated in answering, blushed, and answered that he had come looking for the chief's daughter who knew his name. He asked her of what tribe her father was chief, and where his village was. She answered by pointing to Ouwela, the lake. Then she got up from the fallen tree and gestured for him to follow her toward the lake. He waded through the marshes and penetrated the thickets with difficulty, while the strikingly beautiful maiden made her way without difficulty.

Her path led them into thicket and woods where the only light was an occasional glimmering of twilight through the leaves. They heard the cry of strange birds, and occasionally a snake would slither across the trail in front of them. Eventually, they came to the shore of the lake, where a canoe made of white bark was moored among the water lilies. She stepped into the canoe and pushed off from the shore. She pointed across the dark lake and said that her home was in that direction. She told him that her name was Newamee, and that he should not try to follow her as her canoe moved into the mist.

Owenah continued to visit their place in the woods daily, and he usually found her there. His friends taunted him continually for giving up the hunt and for wandering off by himself. However, the impact of these taunts was more than offset by seeing the object of his affections. He talked with her during the day and dreamed of her at night.

On many occasions, his friends followed him to see how he was spending his time. They were unable to find their old companion. Finally, two young braves penetrated the thicket surrounding the mysterious lake and saw the two of them in the white canoe. However, a black wolf came down the path toward them, and they ran back to the village as fast as they could. Both of these

Newamee as She Reached the Middle of the Lake

braves received serious injuries before the summer was over.

Owenah's bow and arrows hung unused on the wall of his parents' lodge. Summer passed into autumn, and one day Newamee wasn't at their meeting place. There wasn't much mist rising from the haunted lake that day, and he could see the white canoe on the other side of the lake. He called out her name, but the only answer he received was from a bird that seemed to mock him. He thought about some of the things that she had told him: that she lived adjacent to the big sea water, that large lodges floated on the water, and that bottomless Lake Ouwela had a huge cave that led to the big sea waters.

Newamee also told him that she was the daughter of the Great Spirit, and that in time she would send for him. He did not know how to take these revelations, and they filled him with apprehension. The next time that she met him at the lake, she had a very sad look on her face. She told him that he must not come to their meeting place again. She asked him if he had heard the cry of the Kalewee as he walked though the swamp. She told him that the cry of the bird of evil omen was intended as a warning to him.

Owenah placed his hand on Newamee's arm; he said that he wouldn't have to come here anymore if she would agree to marry him and return with him to his lodge. She replied that she could not come to live with Owenah's tribe, because there was a spell on her and she must return home. She reminded him that her home was to the north and that she must return there though the large cave in Lake Ouwela that opened into Seneca Lake and then eventually led to the big sea water. There was nothing she could do to break the spell.

Owenah was stunned; he could not bear the possibility that they might be separated. His voice trembled and he shuddered as he reached out for Newamee. However, she stepped into the canoe and paddled away from the shore. She told him that he couldn't come with him at that time, but that she would talk with the Great Spirit. If He agreed, she said that she would send the white canoe at the time of the next full moon.

As Newamee paddled away from the shore, the sky became dark and thunder could be heard in the distance. Owenah held out his arms and begged her to come back. She said no by shaking her head, and, as she reached the middle of the lake, lightning flashed, thunder boomed, and the winds rose. He saw her disappear, but he could not find her when he waded into the water.

Owenah returned to his village. His family and neighbors could see that he was even more preoccupied than before. He went to the meeting place by the lake every day and called out to Newamee, but he received no reply and saw no white canoe. Finally, he failed to return home. After several days, a search party was sent out for him. They knew that they must risk going through the swamp to the lake to look for him. They found the lifeless Owenah lying in the bottom of a white bark canoe. The Great Spirit had called him to the place by the big sea waters.

The tribe buried him in a mound near Lake Ouwela. The villagers wailed the cry of the dead, "Oonah, Oonah," as they buried him with his little-used weapons. His mother was nearly overcome with sorrow. The villagers visited his grave regularly, even though it was near the haunted lake.

Owenah still rests under the mound near the site of the village of Shinedowa on the plain with Mt. Zoar in the distance. However, his tribe has moved on, leaving little evidence of their stewardship of the land.

The Turtle's Race with the Bear

ne day in early winter, Bear ambled through the woods in a bad mood. He grumbled as he walked by the lakes covered with ice. Bear had not yet learned to hibernate to avoid the winter cold. He walked to the edge of a small lake and hailed Turtle, whose head had poked up through the ice. Bear called Turtle "the slow one." Turtle asked why he was being called "the slow one," and Bear told him that he considered him the slowest of all the creatures. If they raced, Bear laughed, Turtle wouldn't even be in the race.

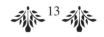

Bear had probably never heard of Turtle's victory in his race with Beaver. Also, Bear may not have been aware that some animals, such as the coyote and the fox, were known more for their wits than their speed. Turtle challenged his furry friend to a race to determine who was the faster. Bear accepted the challenge and asked when and where the race would be held. Turtle told Bear that the race would be just after sunrise the following morning and that Bear would run along the shore of the lake. He, Turtle, would swim in the lake.

Bear asked his encased friend how he was going to swim in the lake when it was covered with ice. Turtle explained that he would punch holes in the ice along the edge of the lake and swim underwater to each hole, where he would stick out his head so Bear would know where he was. Bear agreed to these conditions.

The next morning at daybreak most of the animals of the forest lined the side of the lake to watch. Bear danced around and did some limbering up excercises to prepare himself for the big race. Turtle's head came up through the first hole in the ice, and he announced that he was ready to take on Bear. Bear waddled to the starting point, where he waited for Owl to give a "hoot" to start the race.

Bear started at a brisk pace, causing snow to fly all around him. Turtle's head went down into the water in the first hole in the ice and reappeared at the second hole in an astonishingly short period of time. Turtle taunted his competitor to catch him if he could. Bear's feet pounded even more heavily as he attempted to run faster. However, he saw Turtle's head come up out of the water at the third hole well ahead of him. He looked at Turtle with amazement.

Bear began to huff and puff in his effort to catch up with Turtle. However, he appeared to be losing ground as the race went on. By the time that Bear crossed the finish line, he was exhausted and breathing in gasps. Turtle, and all of his friends of the forest, were waiting for Bear at the end of the race. Bear had not even come close to winning.

Bear was humiliated by his loss, and he couldn't figure out how it had happened. He walked home slowly and heavily, attempting to

deal with his disgrace. He was so exhausted that he slept until the beginning of the spring season. This was the first time that Bear hibernated.

After Bear and all of the other aninals of the forest went home, Turtle tapped on the ice and nine heads looked up from nine holes in the ice. They were Turtle's brothers and cousins; they looked just like him. Turtle thanked his relatives for their help in winning the race with Bear. He pointed out to his brothers and cousins that it is not a good idea to call people names and treat them in a condescending manner. They smiled back at him. They knew that the Turtle is not the slowest of creatures, which was a lesson that Bear learned the hard way.

 ### The Turtle's Race with the Beaver

urtle lived in a shallow pool in a large swamp. The pool, which was surrounded by trees, provided him with a good supply of fish. One hot day, Turtle became drowsy and crawled onto a mud bank, where a stand of reeds provided him with shade from the hot sun. He had a long, deep sleep, and when he awoke he knew that there was something wrong. He was in water that was over his head and over the tops of the reeds in which he had been sleeping. The shallow pool had become a lake.

Turtle swam out to an island made of sticks in the middle of the lake. A dark figure came to the surface of the water from underneath the island. Turtle asked, "Who are you?" Beaver responded, "I am Beaver; I constructed that dam over there and made this lake." Turtle replied that he had been here for a long time, and that the pond was his private fishing spot. He told Beaver that he was going to tear down the dam and return the area to a swamp with a pool. Beaver said that if Turtle destroyed his dam he would build another, and furthermore his relatives would chew off Turtle's head.

Turtle considered ways of settling the disagreement. He pro-

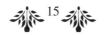

posed that he and Beaver have a contest and that the winner would stay and the loser would leave. Beaver proposed a contest to see who could stay underwater the longest. He knew that he would win, because he could stay submerged for a year. Turtle rejected that idea and suggested that they have a swimming race. Beaver agreed to this proposal and asked Turtle to lay out the course. Turtle suggested that they race from a stump on one side of the lake to a point on the other side of the lake directly across from the stump.

Turtle suggested that he start out behind Beaver, because he was the faster swimmer. Beaver was actually a faster swimmer, but, before he could get too far ahead, Turtle bit down on Beaver's tail. This made Beaver angry, so he swam even faster and began to shake his tail. However, Turtle hung on doggedly; Beaver could not shake him off. Finally, Beaver became so exasperated that he flung his tail over his head with a great heave. Once in the air, Turtle let go of Beaver's tail and was hurled onto the shore of the far side of the lake, winning the race.

Beaver was stunned by losing, because he knew that he was the faster swimmer. Turtle had outwitted him by making him angry. Beaver moved on to another area, and Turtle tore down the dam and reclaimed his private fishing place.

The Turtle's Race With the Beaver

Chapter 2

Evil Legends

The Flying Heads

he nations of the Iroquois Confederation were terrified by the Flying Heads, or Ko-nea-raw-neh, which had long, flaming hair and always appeared with the wind. These repulsive-looking heads were enormous when in motion, but were about the size of the head of a bear on land or in the trees. Some medicine men viewed them as bad spirits, and others thought that their coming foretold terrible calamities. Arrows bounced off them, and everyone fled in terror when they appeared. The Flying Heads would go away for months at a time, and the Iroquois would hope that they had left forever. However, they always returned.

One evening as the sun was going down, an Iroquois squaw, De-wan-do, with her baby wrapped in a blanket and slung across her shoulders, was paddling her canoe across a wide river. As she approached the shore, a large visage with flaming hair rose from the water, causing steam to appear above the surface of the river. She knew about the Flying Heads, so she ran with her infant into the forest where she knew that the game from the previous day's hunt had been stored. She picked up several pieces of venison, which she threw to the Flying Head, one piece at a time, to slow him down. He stopped each time she threw a piece of meat at him, but eventually she ran out of venison.

De-wan-do threw her blanket at the Flying Head; he ripped it to shreds. She then threw her dress made of doe-skin, her leggings, and her moccasins at him as she fled. She was cut and bleeding as she ran unclothed through the brush and briars. Finally, she remembered that an infant's

moccasin could be used as a charm
to ward off danger. She
removed the
moccasin from
one of her child's
feet and flung it at
the Flying Head.
He stopped,
attempted to
avoid the moc-
casin, reeled out
of control, and fell
to the ground.

De-wan-do ran into
the darkest part of the
forest, where she
climbed a tall pine
tree and hid in the
branches. Not real-
izing where she
was, the Flying
Head caught up with
her and fell asleep at
the base of the tree. De-
wan-do climbed down from the tree, but accidentally caused a
large limb to fall on the Flying Head. He was temporarily entan-
gled in the branch but pulled himself clear to pursue De-wan-do.
His flaming hair set fire to the brush that he passed through while
chasing his quarry back to her longhouse.

Famished, De-wan-do roasted some acorns at the hearth, while
her child slept by the fire. She didn't realize that the Flying Head
had entered her lodge and was watching over her shoulder while
she removed the acorns from the fire and ate them. He was surprised by what he saw, because he thought that she was eating the hot coals from the fire. He thought, "They must be good.
I'll have my share." He gobbled many of the hot coals, screamed
in pain, and fled into the woods. A great blaze of fire followed him.
That Flying Head never returned to harass the village.

The Legend of Hi'non

i'non, the God of Thunder, was one of the great, good gods of the Iroquois. He was considered second in importance only to the Great Spirit; in some histories of the Iroquois, the God of Thunder and the Great Spirit were considered to be one being. The God of Thunder, or He-great-voice, was the maker of rain and storms. When he wrinkled his forehead, thunder would be heard. When he blinked his eyes, lightning would shoot toward the earth.

The God of Thunder was an enemy of all evil spirits. He intimidated the malevolent beings of the underworld and forced them to return to their caves. His goal was to kill all malicious creatures that used evil magic and to slay the underwater serpent.

One of the legends about Hi'non involved his pursuit of the evil serpent that was poisoning the springs of a tribe that lived to the west of the Finger Lakes Region. The monster serpent was the length of twenty arrow flights. The malicious serpent lived underground along a river and would come out at night and spread his poison into the tribe's drinking water. Hi'non found the serpent spreading destruction one night and killed him with bolts of lightning that were like arrows of fire. The huge serpent squirmed and twisted in pain.

The men of the tribe dragged the writhing, nearly spent body of the evil serpent to the river and threw him in. In his death throes, he flailed over the precipice of a waterfall, enlarging it and changing its shape forever.

The Lost Onondaga Babe

reen Lake, called Kai-yah-koo by the Onondagas, is located in Fayetteville, Onondaga County. Just under 200 feet deep, the lake is appropriately named. Its unique green color is due to its small amount of plant life and the presence of minimal suspended material in the water.

The legend begins with Laque, an Onondaga squaw, walking along the shore of the clear, deep lake returning to her village from a visit to Oneida Castle. She was carrying her eight-month-old son and supplies for which she had bartered at Oneida Castle. It was a hot day of the seventh moon as she walked the trail along the lake. As dusk approached, Laque stopped along the shore lined with marl- and moss-covered rocks. She looked forward to a rest as she removed the burden's trumpline across her forehead and rested her papoose against the root of a tree.

Laque lapsed wearily into a dream. She heard a noise in the bushes nearby and wondered if it was a wild animal or a devil of the evening. Then she saw a well-dressed woman emerge from the thicket. The stranger looked at Laque's baby and placed an infant that she carried on the ground next to him.

The beautiful woman told Laque of a difficult journey from her village to the south. She was a princess, the only daughter of a powerful sachem, and she had displeased her father and been cast out from her tribe. Her father had killed her husband and intended to slay her child as well. She was exhausted from her journey. The stranger's voice was so soft and melodic that Laque was mesmerized by it. Laque was strongly moved by sympathy for the princess.

The richly dressed woman reminded Laque that the customs of their nation did not prevent the exchanging of children. She asked Laque to take her child, and said that she would take Laque's infant and raise him as her own. That way, her father would not attempt to kill the substituted child. At some point in the future, they could exchange the children back to their rightful parents. Laque saw that precious gems decorated the clothing of the son of the princess, and that he had eyes that sparkled brightly. Laque, who was tired and not thinking clearly, agreed to the exchange.

The princess quickly picked up Laque's infant and lifted him onto her shoulder. The infant smiled at Laque as the stranger carried him off into the forest. Laque placed the exchanged infant on her back and continued her journey. She thought that she could hear her own son crying in the woods. Laque had been on the trail only a short time when she felt a clawing and scratching on her back. Her blanket was torn from her shoulders, and the back of her doeskin dress was ripped.

Laque removed the papoose from her back and found that the fancy clothing with the glistening gems was gone, and, instead of an infant, a young alligator returned her stare. She pushed the alligator away and fell to the ground exhausted, confused, and nearly unconscious. Laque came to her senses in the middle of night. By the light of the moon and the stars, she returned to the shore of Green Lake and called out for her son. In despair, the broken-hearted woman cried out until daybreak.

She climbed up to one of the higher elevations around the lake and looked down into the ravine below; she considered leaping into the chasm and taking her own life. As she asked for the forgiveness of the Great Spirit, she heard a voice say "live." She trudged along the path back to her village. She entered her lodge and tearfully told her husband what had happened. He replied that it was obviously the work of an evil spirit. They visited the village's medicine man, the oracle of their nation, to ask what they should do. He told them to return in three days for his answer.

The oracle told them that their child was taken by the evil spirit, O-nee-hoo-hugh-noo, who had assumed the form of a beautiful woman. However, the Great Spirit has heard the cry of their son and has taken away the power of the wicked spirit. Furthermore, the oracle told them that their infant would be safe and would not be injured in any way. He told them to go up upon a high bank nearby if they wanted to hear their son. The medicine man told them that they would never get him back, but that he would be happy with the Great Spirit.

He also told them that the Good Spirit, Ha-wah-ne-u, had asked that they give an offering of tobacco each year to ensure the guardian's care of their child. He told them to stand on a high ledge above Green Lake and to cast the tobacco into the clear waters below. He said that the first time that they did this, the serpent would be driven away and they would be bothered no more. When they climbed up to the ledge, they saw a huge monster, about sixty feet long, in a threatening pose. The serpent raised his head above

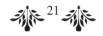

the surface of the water and spewed fire and smoke toward them. However, they were too far away to feel threatened by the monster.

The couple threw a large amount of tobacco in the lake that spread over a broad expanse of its surface. The color of the lake took on a green hue, and the serpent disappeared. The Great Spirit had broken the spell of the evil spirit and had banished the monster forever. Laque and her husband offered tobacco every year. The Onondaga name for the lake, Kai-yah-koo, which means "satisfied with tobacco," is derived from this ceremony. The custom was still being observed when the first white men entered the region.

Throwing Tobacco on the Serpent in Green Lake

Chapter 3

General Legends

The Four Iroquois Hunters

One winter long ago, four Iroquois hunters spent the winter trapping instead of hunting. They were very successful, and, at the end of the winter when they brought their furs to the trading post, they bought all of the things that their families needed. They even had enough left over to buy a rifle.

Although the four braves hunted and trapped together and were all members of the Bear Clan, they belonged to different Iroquois nations. One hunter was from the Seneca Nation, also called the Nundawaono or People of the Great Hill. The second hunter was a Cayuga, the Gueugwehono or People of the Mucky Land. Another was an Onondaga, also known as the Onundagaono or People of the Hills. The fourth hunter was a Mohawk, called the Ganeagaono or People of the Flint.

When they were ready to return to their homes, they divided evenly the items that they had purchased at the trading post. They were confronted with a problem. They couldn't divide up the rifle; they had to decide which of them would take it. The four braves decided that the one who could tell the tallest story about hunting would take the rifle back to his longhouse.

The Mohawk told a story about a hunter who had been in the forests all day hunting with an old muzzle loader. He had used all of his bullets and had nothing to show for it. He picked cherries off a cherry tree in his path and spit the pits into his hand as he walked along. He saw a magnificent buck directly in front him, so he loaded his gun with gunpowder and the cherry pits and fired at the deer's head. The buck fell but got back up and ran away.

A few years later, the brave was hunting in the same part of the forest when he saw a cherry tree loaded with fruit. He leaned his gun against the tree and climbed it to reach the cherries. The tree began to shake, and it was lifted up into the air. The hunter was thrown out of the tree. From his position on the ground, he saw that the tree was growing out of the head of an immense buck. The deer shook his head and the huge rack of antlers one more time and ran into the forest. That ended the Mohawk's story.

The Onondaga brave told a story about his uncle hunting in the woods. He only had one shot left in his rifle, and he wanted to make it count. He walked up to bank along a brook and saw a duck swimming back and forth. Beyond the duck was large rainbow trout jumping out of the water catching flies. A deer stood across the brook and looked around warily. Behind the deer on a small hill was a bear standing on his hind legs rubbing his claws on the bark of a tree.

The Onondaga's uncle sprawled on his stomach, aimed, and, when the trout jumped and the targets were all lined up, fired his last bullet. The bullet went through the trout and killed the duck. The bullet ricocheted off the surface of the water and passed through the deer and killed the bear. When his uncle turned the bear over to skin it, he found that it had fallen on a fox and killed it. Furthermore, the fox had a plump rabbit in his mouth.

The Cayuga told the next story, one about his grandfather hunting deer. His grandfather saw a deer in front of him, and he ran so fast that he couldn't slow down and ran right by the deer. The deer jumped over a brook to get away, but the experienced hunter jumped the stream just behind the scared deer. When the grandfather was halfway across the brook, he saw that he wasn't going to be able to reach the other side, so he turned around in midair and landed back on the side from which he had jumped.

The deer hid behind a hill on the other side of the stream. The grandfather was angry with himself for letting the buck get away. He placed his rifle between two sturdy trees that were close together and bent the barrel downward. Then he fired at the deer and the bullet curved over the top of the hill and struck the deer. The grandfather went to the other side of the hill and immediately began to skin the buck. He pulled the skin toward the antlers to remove it from the body. However, the deer was not dead, and he jumped up and tried to run away. When the hunter tried to grab the deer, he couldn't hold on because the deer was too slippery. As the buck ran away, his skin got caught on the bark of a shagbark hickory tree and came off over his antlers. The grandfather was left with only the skin for his troubles. The Cayuga brave said that if they wanted to verify his story, they could go to his grandfather's longhouse. The skin of the deer was hanging on the wall there.

The Seneca hunter's turn to tell a story had come. He paused and looked at his fellow hunters. Then he smiled and shook his head. He apologized and told them that Seneca braves never tell tall stories about hunting. His three companions looked at one another and, without comment, handed the rifle to the Seneca.

How the Bear Lost His Tail

Bear used to have a long, black, glossy tail. He was very proud of it, and he would flaunt it by waving it around to attract attention. Fox noticed how proud Bear was of his most prized possession. Fox was known as a trickster who loved to fool the other animals; he decided to play one of his tricks on Bear.

It was wintertime, and Hatho, the Spirit of Frost, had descended upon the land covering lakes with ice and weighing down the trees with snow. Fox made a hole in the ice near the path that Bear used every day. He caught many long perch and fat trout and placed them around the hole. Bear walked by and greeted Fox, who asked him how he was. Bear said that he was well and asked Fox what he was doing. Fox pulled his tail out of the water with a large trout hanging onto it, and said that he was fishing; he asked Bear if he would like to try.

Bear said that he would and began to walk over to Fox's hole in the ice. Fox pointed out that this particular hole had been fished out, but he offered to cut a new hole for Bear to use in catching many perch and trout. Fox took Bear over to a place that he knew

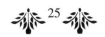

25

was too shallow to catch fish during the winter. The fish always moved to deeper water when Hatho covered the lake with ice and snow.

Fox cut the new hole in the ice and told Bear to do what he said. He instructed Bear to be very quiet, to face away from the hole, and to drop his tail into the water. Fox told him that soon a fish will come along and grab his tail, and he should then pull the fish out of the water. Bear asked how he would know that a fish had grabbed his tail, since his back was to the hole. Fox told him that he would hide many feet away where the fish could not see him, and that he would shout when the fish had latched onto his tail. Then he instructed Bear to pull on his tail as hard as he could. Fox told Bear to be patient and not to move until he instructed him to do so.

Bear followed Fox's instructions to the letter. Once Fox had observed that Bear had followed his directions exactly, he went home and went to bed. When Fox woke up the next morning, his first thoughts were of Bear. He wondered if Bear was still sitting on the ice with his tail in the water. Fox returned to the lake and saw what appeared to be a pile of snow on the ice next to the hole that he had cut in the ice for Bear. Bear had fallen asleep and had been covered with snow by Hatho. Bear was snoring so loudly that he would have scared away the fish if any had been nearby. Fox laughed so much that he could hardly stay on his feet.

Fox walked over next to Bear and yelled into his ear that he had caught a fish. Bear awakened immediately and pulled on his tail as hard as he could. His tail had been frozen solid in the shallow water, and, when he pulled hard, the tail broke off in the ice. Bear looked around to see the fish that he had caught and saw his tail stuck in the ice instead.

Bear told Fox that he would get even with him for this trick. However, Fox could run much faster than Bear and never felt threatened by his much larger adversary. That is why bears have short tails, and why they do not like foxes. They remember the nasty trick that was played on them for which they have never taken revenge.

How the Chipmunk Got His Stripes

long time ago, a bear was walking through the forest, thinking very highly of himself. He was big and strong and felt confident that he could do whatever he chose to do. In fact, he said out loud, "There is nothing that I cannot do." He heard a small voice respond, "Is that so?" The bear looked down and saw a small chipmunk looking up out of a hole in the ground. The bear said, "I can do anything." He then pushed a large log aside with a light touch of his paw, and reminded the chipmunk that all of the animals were afraid of him.

The chipmunk asked the bear, "Can you stop the sun from rising in the morning?" The bear admitted that he had never tried, but he bragged that he could if he wanted to. The chipmunk asked the bear if he was sure, and he said, "Tomorrow morning the sun will not rise." The bear sat down facing east to wait for morning to come. The chipmunk returned to his hole to sleep, while laughing at the bear for his foolishness.

Early in the morning, the bear glared at the light forming in the East and said, "The sun will not rise today." Of course, as always, the sun rose

at dawn. The chipmunk climbed out of his hole and laughed at the bear. Then he began to taunt the bear, while running around singing little ditties that belittled the bear. The chipmunk laughed so hard that he collapsed and rolled onto his back. The bear quickly placed a paw on the little mocker, pinning him to the ground. The bear pointed out that he might not be able to prevent the sun from rising, but that the chipmunk would not live to see another sunrise.

The chipmunk began to compliment the bear and tell him how strong and how quick he was, particularly when he was scooping trout from the stream. He told the bear that he had only been kidding. But the bear did not remove his paw from the chest of his taunter. The chipmunk acknowledged that the bear had the right to kill him, but he pleaded for the opportunity to say one last prayer. Bear told him to pray quickly, because the end of his time on earth had come.

The chipmunk told his tormentor that his paw was pressing on his chest so heavily that he couldn't breathe, let alone say a prayer. The bear lifted his paw slightly, and the chipmunk darted for his hole. The bear wasn't quick enough to stop the chipmunk, but his claws scratched three scars down his back. When the scars healed, they left three stripes on the back of the chipmunk. They serve as a reminder of what can happen when one animal teases another, particularly when the teaser is smaller than the teased.

Chapter 4

Ethereal Legends

The Boy Who Lived with the Bears

Hono', a young Iroquois boy, was an unloved and unwanted stepson. His stepfather yelled at him frequently, never complimented him for anything that he did, and complained that he ate too much. Hono' promised to hunt for food for the family when he was old enough to repay his stepfather. He asked his stepfather if he would like him then. His mean step-parent merely growled at him.

The stepfather began to plot ways of ridding himself of his stepson. He devised a plan to pretend that he was friendly with the child. He suggested to Hono' that it was time that he begin to learn how to hunt and invited him on a hunting trip. The young boy was delighted to be invited, and he accepted without hesitation.

They traveled for a considerable distance through the thicket. Hono' asked his stepfather why they were going though the bushes instead of into the woods where the tribe's hunters went. His stepfather told him not to worry; he was a good hunter and knew of a good place to go. Hono' asked why he didn't have a bow and quiver of arrows with which to hunt. He was told that they would come later.

After walking for several miles, his stepfather stopped, feigned surprise, and said, "Look. There is a hole. Hurry, Hono', crawl in there and catch the game. You can be a big hunter now!" Hono' was happy that he could do something to please his stepparent, so he crawled in willingly. He moved on his hands and knees down the long tunnel until he could no longer see clearly. He began to return to where the daylight was still shining in and was surprised to see the opening of the tunnel grow dark. When he arrived at the opening he was astounded to find that a large rock had been rolled in place to close the entry to the tunnel.

Outside, the perpetrator of this ruse was laughing to himself at how easy the deception had been and was thinking, "Hono' will never be able to push aside that large boulder." Hono' was dazed by what his stepfather had done. He knew that his stepfather didn't like him, but he didn't think that he would go to this extreme to get rid of him.

Hono' heard voices coming from outside the entrance to the cavern. He could hear a meeting in which his name was mentioned frequently. Someone pulled the boulder away from the opening and called for him to come out of the tunnel. He emerged into the daylight outside of the cave and saw a large gathering of animals sitting in a circle. A porcupine was asking, "Now that the boy has been saved, who will care for him?" All of the animals began to speak at once, and all of them offered to care for him. The porcupine said, "Hold! Everyone cannot take care of him. Let each of us tell the boy of our living habits, our temperament, and the food that we eat, and let him chose which of us will be his guardian."

All of the animals described why it would be to the boy's advantage to live with them. Finally, the bear said, "I am old and rather surly, but I have a warm heart. I live happily in summer and sleep much in winter. I eat honey, nuts, and berries." As soon as the bear had stopped talking, Hono' exclaimed, "I would like to live with the bear family." The boy was amazed at the gathering of the animals. They acted as though they were humans instead of animals, and they all talked the same language. He knew that some of them were each other's enemies, but they behaved well during the discussion.

The bear led Hono' to her family's den. She told him, "I wish you to become my grandson, because I have lost one and wish you to take his place and drive away my sorrow." They arrived at a hollow tree and mother bear took Hono' by the neck and lowered him into her den. He looked around and saw that their quarters were very comfortable. Hono' shared the bear family's meals of honeycombs and dried berries.

His foster grandmother introduced him to her two grandsons. Hono' was happy that he would have playmates in his new home. He found his two foster brothers to be very rambunctious, and they pushed him around frequently. However, he pushed them back in return, and they played well together.

When summer came, Hono' and the two young cubs offered to help with the gathering of berries to store for the coming winter. Grandmother bear told Hono' of the problems that they always had when they picked berries. Hunters, unfriendly animals, and large birds of prey tried to attack them in the berry patch. She told Hono' that she planned to dress him as a warrior, to paint his face, and to provide him with a bow and a quiver of arrows. She told him that if any of their enemies appeared to whoop and holler and shoot his arrows at them.

Hono' accompanied them to the berry fields and shot many of his arrows. However, most of his targets were birds. The berry season was followed by autumn, the season in which the bears gathered nuts for the next winter. Grandmother bear reminded them that this was a dangerous time for bears, because of the many hunters in the woods. Also there were many fruit and root gatherers in the fields in the fall.

Hono' in the tunnel

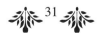

They didn't see any human hunters for many days. Finally, they saw one in the distance. Grandmother bear called him a Do-sko-a-o, or brush-in-the-mouth hunter. The hunter was chewing a pine twig, which gave off a scent that provided the bears with an advance warning of his presence. The bears hid in a hollow tree, and the hunter walked by without finding them. Another type of hunter was the heavy stepper, who tromped around in the forest warning everyone of his approach. A third type was the "swinging mouth," who warned everyone by humming or singing as he walked through the woods.

When Hono' and the bears were returning to their den, grand-mother bear saw a real hunter coming. They called this hunter "four eyes" because he hunted with a dog. She knew that they were in trouble because very little escaped the attention of this hunter or his dog. She recognized him as Hono's stepfather. She told Hono' that if his stepfather chopped down the hollow tree in which they were hiding, she would leave the tree first, followed by the two cubs and Hono'.

Hono's stepfather set a fire at the base of the tree. He kept cutting the coals of the burned bark away so the flames could devour the dry wood behind the coals. When the tree crashed to the ground, grandmother bear ran away first but was stopped by an arrow through the heart; however, her ghost-body ran on. Hono's stepfather also shot the two cubs as they tried to escape. Hono' crawled out of the fallen tree and cried out to his stepfather, "Are you going to shoot me too?"

Hono's stepfather asked the boy what he had done since he had left him, and inquired what he was doing hiding in the tree with the bears. His stepfather apologized for being unkind to him and for killing his friends. He told Hono' that if he had called out, he would not have killed the bears. He was afraid of the bear ghosts, and thought that now he would always have bad luck. Hono' told him not to worry because now he, Hono', could be useful around the lodge and could hunt. Hono' asked him if he would like him now that he could be useful. His stepfather replied, "Truly." The stepfather never hunted again; Hono' did the hunting for them.

The Legend of the Star Maidens

Many years ago, a brave was walking along a river to the west of the Finger Lakes Region when he found a clearing marked with a circular path formed by the tread of many moccasined feet. He recognized immediately that it was a ring made by the Star Maidens when they came down to earth from Sky Land. That night when the moon—called the Sister of the Sun by the Native Americans—was high in the heavens, the brave hid in the tall grass near the clearing. He could hear soft music playing in the distance.

The brave looked up and saw a small white cloud in the sky that appeared to be moving toward the earth. When it came closer, he saw that it was a willow basket containing twelve beautiful maidens. The basket landed softly in the tall grass nearby, and the maidens stepped out of their conveyance and into the magic circle in the clearing. They danced with such grace and precision that the brave was captivated.

His gaze focused on the youngest of the twelve, who appeared to be the most beautiful. The brave, who had decided to ask the delicate young maiden to be his bride, rushed from the tall grass toward the dancing sisters. However, she quickly ran from him toward the willow basket. Before he could stop them, all of the maidens had climbed into the basket and were wafted upward toward Sky Land.

The brave returned again the next night and, using some of his tribal magic, turned himself into a tree. The Star Maidens returned, and, as they danced, the youngest sister ventured near to the tree. The brave turned back into his human form and, taking the maiden into his arms, carried her back to his lodge. He was very tender with her, and soon she returned his love and accepted his marriage proposal. Although her marriage was blessed by the birth of a son, she still missed her sisters, her parents, and her friends. One day she wove a basket out of willow and, taking her young son with her, returned to Sky Land.

The brave was overcome with grief. Every day he returned to the circle in the clearing, hoping to see his wife again. Eventually, when their son had grown into a strong young brave, she returned with him to Earth Land. Her husband was overjoyed. He was so happy to be reunited that he agreed to return with them to Sky Land. Before they set off to the heavens, she told him to bring a feather from every bird and a claw or bone from every animal that he had killed in the hunt.

He took this collection with him when he was transported skyward with his wife and son. Upon their arrival in Sky Land, the brave distributed the bones, claws, and feathers. Everyone who received a bone or claw turned into that animal. Those to whom he gave a feather were changed into a bird. The brave, his wife, and his son each took a feather from the white wood dove. They were all changed into that beautiful bird and flew down to earth where their descendants can be seen today.

 ## The Legend of the Sun, the Moon, and the Morning Star

he Iroquois considered the Sun, the Moon, and the Morning Star to be gods that exerted influence and power over human destiny. They thought that the Sun was created by the Earth Mother who had given birth to the twins, Good-minded and Bad-minded, who in turn, created humans, animals, birds, fish, trees, and all other living things. Native Americans considered the Sun a god of war and the messenger of the Sky Chief. The Sun rested in the Celestial Tree in Sky Land, rose in the eastern sky, and watched over the daily activities of the people below. In the evening, Sun returned to his place of repose in Sky Land and told Sky Chief all that he had observed on earth that day.

Moon was known as Grandmother / Grandfather, the most mysterious of all the bodies in the heavens. She was followed by the braves for signs of good luck with the hunt. She was also worshipped by the squaws, who prayed to her for the good health of the tribe.

Morning Star was also thought to be one of the principal beings in the sky and could be viewed as either feminine or masculine. Her appearance in the morning sky was recognized as an omen, either for good or for evil. As a good omen, she was seen as the rescuer of starving families during famine. As an evil omen, she was envisioned as an enchantress who lured hunters from their path and then left them to wander around lost.

The Sun, the Moon, and the Morning Star were but three of the many influences on the Iroquois. Other influences include the Frost God, the Spirit of Spring, the Storm Wind, and the Winter Spirit.

Chapter 5

Native Origin Legends

The Origin of All Legends

Many years ago when a young Seneca orphan boy grew to be tall and strong, his foster mother gave him a bow and arrow and told him that it was his responsibility to keep the family provided with birds and small game. One afternoon, as he rested on a large rock, he heard a voice ask him if he would like to hear stories of the Senecas who had lived before him.

The young boy looked around, but he couldn't see anybody. Then he realized that the voice was coming from the rock on which he was sitting. The voice asked him to leave as an offering the birds that he had killed earlier that day. The voice told stories of adventures and battles and tales of the flying heads and the stone giants. The boy was fascinated. The voice stopped at sundown, and the young orphan left his birds at the rock and started home to his lodge.

He shot more birds on the way home, but he had so few when he arrived that his foster mother scolded him. The next day, he went to the rock again and again left the birds that he had killed as an offering. He told some of his friends about the voice from the rock, and they went with him. They also left small game as an offering at the rock and were enthralled with the stories told by the mysterious voice.

On the following day, two braves followed the boys to see why they had brought home so little game from their hunting trips. As soon as the voice began to speak from the rock, the two braves came out from their hiding place and listened with the boys. That evening, the braves told the chief about the stories, and, on the following day, the entire tribe came to hear them. They brought offerings of cornbread and venison. The Senecas listened attentively to the stories emanating from the rock. At the end of the day, the voice invited them to come back the following day.

When they returned the next morning, The Voice of the Rock continued with the stories for what was to be the last time. At sunset, the voice told them to remember the stories well, because he would not return. The voice encouraged them to pass the stories on from generation to generation; he would not be telling them again. That was the source of the Seneca legends. The nation's storytellers have been telling them ever since.

The Legend of the Pipe of Peace

The peace pipe was always smoked at Iroquois councils at which treaties were made. The practice of smoking the pipe of peace was originated years ago by a Iroquois sachem who possessed considerable wisdom and good judgment. He traveled among the tribes of the Iroquois Confederation promoting peace. He advised them to be charitable and to aid one another. He counseled those who were blessed with plenty to help those who were less fortunate.

This astute sachem attended all councils of war and councils to settle disputes among tribes. His sage advice facilitated the way to peaceful settlements. By offering a good example and by applying sound judgment, he settled disagreements and averted war. Among the nations of the Iroquois Confederation, he became known as the Peacemaker. When he grew old and frail, he gathered his people around him and told them that he was going to join the Great Spirit in Sky Land. He told them not to be concerned, because he would reappear in another form and continue to be with them forever.

After the death of the wise sachem, one of the chiefs found an unusual plant growing in front of the Peacemaker's lodge. They heard the voice of the Peacemaker saying that this strange plant was the tobacco plant, the form in which he was reappearing to them. He told them to smoke this new plant in pipes made of stone.

He also advised that they pass the Pipe of Peace around in their councils in memory of him.

The custom was established of smoking the Pipe of Peace at all councils. The chiefs believed that they could envision the Peacemaker in the smoke that wafted upward from their stone pipes. He had told them always to keep commitments that they made in his presence. The Iroquois never broke a promise accompanied by the passing of the Pipe of Peace.

The Legend of the Origin of Wampum

An Iroquois brave walking through the forest saw a huge bird covered with a heavy coating of wampum. He ran home to his village and told his chief and the people of the village what he had seen. They thought that the bird came from another world, and the chief offered the hand of his daughter in marriage to the brave who could capture it, dead or alive.

Armed with bows and arrows, the braves of the village went to the "tree of promise" and shot at the enormous bird. Some of the arrows barely scraped the wampum covering the bird. As the arrows caused large amounts of wampum to fall to the ground, new wampum—like Hydra's heads—was created. None of the warriors were able to kill the bird or to wound him so that he would have to come down to earth.

A small boy from a neighboring tribe came to see the wondrous bird that everyone was discussing. His tribe was at war with the braves who were attempting to shoot the bird. The braves did not allow him to shoot at the bird; in fact, they threatened him with death if he did. Finally, their chief said, "He is a mere boy; let him shoot on equal terms with you who are brave and fearless warriors." The boy, displaying more skill with bow and arrow than the mature braves, brought the target to the ground with one shot.

The boy received the hand of the chief's daughter in marriage, the wampum was split evenly between the two tribes, and peace was declared between them. The new husband declared that wampum should from then on be the price of blood and peace, and that all thoughts of vengence should be set aside. This declaration was adopted by all nations of the Iroquois Confederation. This was the origin of the custom of giving belts of wampum for reasons of hospitality, satisfaction of violated honor, and the encouragement of peace between nations.

Chapter 6

Destiny Legends

The Legend of the Door at Taughannock

When observing the 215-foot-high falls from the overlook in Taughannock Falls State Park, visitors can envision the outline of a door high on the wall of the ravine to the right of the waterfall. The Iroquois considered it a mystery of nature that they could not explain, so they created a legend about it.

Chief Ganungueguch and his tribe lived along Taughannock Creek in the area of the waterfall many years before the white man entered the region. The Iroquois were continually at war with the Delawares from Pennsylvania. Chief Taughannock and his Delawares raided the Cayugas and Senecas in the region and were defeated. Chief Taughannock and most of his braves were killed, but some of the Delawares survived and were adopted by their captors.

One of the adopted Delaware braves fell in love with White Lily, a Cayuga maiden. The Cayuga braves were jealous and watched the pair closely to prevent them from running away together. One dark night, the two lovers ran toward the Delaware's canoe on the shore of Cayuga Lake. They planned to escape southward to Delaware country. An early alarm frustrated their attempt to escape. They didn't know whether a jealous brave gave the alarm, or the barking of one of the tribe's dogs alerted the village. Soon the entire village was chasing them through the pine forest adjacent to the village.

From the shouts of the braves in pursuit, the couple knew that they would be overtaken before reaching the ford across the creek above the falls. They ran from the protection of the pine forest and could be seen in the moonlight. They stood on the edge of the falls, embaced,

and leapt to what they thought was certain death on the jagged
rocks below. They preferred death to capture and the torture that
would be inflicted on the Delaware brave according to the code of
the Iroquois.

The villagers gathered near the pinnacle from which the two
had jumped, and the squaws of the tribe wailed at the death of the
maiden. When the lamentations subsided, the people returned to
the village. They planned to return to the base on the falls to bury
the young couple in the morning.

When the villagers returned to the site of the young people's
death after dawn, however, they found no mangled bodies or any
trace of the brave and the maiden. The tribe's storytellers said that
the Great Spirit was aware of the young couple's love and of their
attempt to elope. The Great Spirit sympathized with them. He
opened the door high on the side of the ravine, and when they
jumped he ushered them through the secret passageway and closed
the door tightly. The passageway led to a domain where White Lily
and her Delaware lover could live in peace and happiness forever.

 ### The Maid Who Fell in Love with the Morning Star

One night a beautiful Iroquois maiden slept outside the door of her lodge on sleeping robes that
she had spread in the tall grass. While she slept, a shaft of light
from above fell upon her face and seemed to touch her gently.
When she awoke, she realized the the light had come from the
Morning Star up above in Sky Land.

The caress of the tender glow moved her so deeply that she fell
in love with the source of the silvery radiance from the heavens.
She made a pledge that she would never marry a mere mortal; she
would marry the Morning Star or not marry at all. She stared
upward toward Sky Land every night until the brightness of the sun
caused the light of her jewel in the heavens to fade. She watched
her celestial lover each night and thought about him each day.

Indian Woman Transfigured into Weeping Willow

One morning she went to a spring near her lodge and was surprised to encounter a handsome brave whom she did not know. He smiled when he told her that he was the Morning Star. He said that he knew that she had been looking at him, and that he also knew what was in her heart. He asked her to marry him, and she accepted his proposal. Morning Star removed a long, yellow plume from his hair and handed it to her. As soon as she grasped it in her hand, she was lifted into Sky Land where she was welcomed into Morning Star's lodge.

She lived in her husband's lodge in comfort and was free to go anywhere that she chose. Her only restriction was that she was not to go near a strange golden plant that grew outside of their lodge. One day she couldn't contain her curiousity any longer, and she pulled the plant out of the ground to see what was beneath it. She found that the hole through which she had entered Sky Land was underneath the curious plant. When she looked through the hole, she could see the people of her village on earth below. She could hear the voices of her friends. She became very homesick and began to cry.

Morning Star found her weeping and knew immediately what she had done. He commanded her to return to her people. She returned to earth on the strands of silvery web like a strong spider web. Her exile from Sky Land saddened her, and each evening she walked up a nearby hill, lifted her arms skyward, and begged to be united with her husband.

One evening Morning Star responded to her prayers. He told her that she could never be forgiven; she would never allowed to return to Sky Land. She was deeply saddened to hear this, and the next day she could not be found. The villagers searched the top of the hill, but she had disappeared. They found a tree growing on the spot where she had lifted her arms skyward in prayer. They were not familar with the strange tree whose branches seemed to droop downward in sadness. We know the tree as the weeping willow.

The Legend of the Violets

A young Iroquois chief served his tribe heroically by accomplishing three things. He had slain the great bird of prey that had swept down from the sky and flown away with small children while they were at play. He had traveled alone to the mysterious witches' caves and obtained magic medicine to save his village from a deadly plague, without knowing whether he would be allowed to return. Finally, he led the braves of his tribe to an overwhelming victory over their most powerful enemy, while distinguishing himself by his leadership and valour.

When he had attacked his enemy's village, he had seen the daughter of their chief and was captivated by her. However, he realized that as long as the two tribes were at war, he could not offer the presents of a suitor, such as fur robes or wampum. He hid in the forest near her village just to see her from a distance. He sang her praises aloud so many times that the birds copied his song. The bear and the fox heard him talk in his sleep of the maiden's charms so often that they thought he was speaking of a beautiful flower.

One day the young maiden ventured out beyond the boundary of her village, and the young chief took her into his arms and ran away with her through the woods toward his village. One of the braves of the maiden's village saw her being carried off and sounded an alarm. The braves from the village tracked the young chief and the maiden and caught up with them the next morning.

The maiden had fallen in love with her captor and was now a willing captive. To show the pursuing braves that she wanted to marry the young chief, she stood next to him with the braids of her hair entwined around his neck—indicating that, according to custom, the two young people wanted to marry. The pursuing braves were incensed by her response and killed the two young lovers where they stood, with the maiden's hair still encircling her intended's neck.

The braves left them, and when they returned the next morning the bodies had disappeared. On the spot where they had been struck down, two clusters of violets grew. People of the village had not seen the fragrant flowers before. Birds carried the seeds of the violets to other countries where young people have the courage to love in spite of obstacles.

Chapter 7

Self-Sacrifice Legends

The Legend of Lelawala

Many years ago, a peaceful Native American tribe lived by a waterfall to the west of the Finger Lakes Region. They called the waterfall Thunderer of the Waters and thought that its roar was the voice of the Great Spirit. The tribe had a custom of offering their fairest maiden to the Great Spirit as a sacrifice every year. Chosen at a formal ceremony, she was honored to represent the tribe and thanked the Great Spirit for being selected.

Lelawala, the daughter of Chief Eagle Eye, was the last maiden to be sacrificed. On the day that she was to be offered up, she appeared on the river bank upstream from the Thunderer of the Waters. She was dressed in white doeskin and wore a garland of wild flowers on her head. The older squaws of the tribe accompanied her.

Lelawala stepped willingly into her white birch canoe that had been filled with woodland flowers, waved good-bye to her family and friends, and paddled out into the swift flowing river. Many young braves looked at her wistfully. Her canoe was propelled by the rapids to the edge of the waterfall, and she was hurled over the brink to her death.

Chief Eagle Eye watched from the riverbank with the rest of the tribe. He did not cry out, because he knew that his daughter was following the traditions of her people. However, he felt a great anguish, and his heart was broken. Before anyone could stop him, he jumped into his canoe and paddled out into the river. The rapids carried him swiftly over the waterfall where he joined his daughter in death. According to legend, Lelawala and her father live in a cave behind the waterfall. The tribe discontinued their annual sacrifice; they were a peaceful people, and the losses of Lelawala and her father were too great for them to bear.

The Sacrifice of Aliquipiso

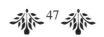

n Oneida village was raided by a band of Mingoes from the North. The Mingoes had listened to bad spirits, and they killed everyone and destroyed or plundered everything in their path. The Oneida women and children abandoned their lodges and fled to the large rocks in the hills, where their their braves protected them. The savage marauders searched for days without success for the people of the village.

The Oneidas began to run out of food; they feared that if they foraged and hunted, they would be killed. Meeting in council, the warriors and chiefs could think of no solution to their problems. If they remained behind the rocks on the cliff, they would starve; if they ventured out, they would be enslaved or brutally murdered.

A young maiden, Aliquipiso, visited the council of braves and sachems and told them of an idea that the good spirits had given to her. They told her that if the rocks high on the cliff were rolled into the valley below, everything there would be destroyed. The good spirits also told Aliquipiso that if she would lure the plundering Mingoes to the valley below the rocks, they would be killed also. The braves and chiefs were relieved to hear of a solution to their troubles. They gave her a necklace of white wampum, made her a princess of the Oneida Nation, and reminded her that she was loved by the Great Spirit.

Aliquipiso left her people in the middle of the night and climbed down from the cliff. The next morning, Mingo scouts found a young maiden wandering around lost in the forest. They led Aliquipiso back to the abandoned Oneida village, where they attempted to get her to reveal the hiding place of the Oneidas. They tortured her; she held out a long time and won the respect of her captors. Finally, she told the Mingoes that she would lead them to her people. When darkness came, Aliquipiso led her captors to the base of the cliff. Two strong Mingo braves held her in their grasp and were prepared to take her life at the first hint of deceit.

All of the warriors gathered around Aliquipiso, thinking that she was going to show them an opening into a large cave in the cliff. Suddenly, she lifted her head and let out a piercing cry—a forewarning of death. Above them, the starving Oneida braves pushed the large boulders over the cliff. The Mingoes did not have time to get out the way and were crushed under the large rocks, along with the Oneida heroine.

Aliquipiso, who was buried near the scene of her courageous sacrifice, was mourned by the Oneidas for many moons. The Great Spirit used her hair to create woodbine, called "running hairs" by the Iroquois, the climbing vine that protects old trees. The Great Spirit changed her body into honeysuckle, which was called "the blood of brave women" by the Oneidas.

The Tree of the Silver Arrows

 Seneca father and his two sons left their long-house to travel to the edge of the earth and then across Crystal Lake to the Land of the Great Spirit. On the shore of the large lake, they encountered three eagles, who offered to convey them across the waters. The three Senecas rode the backs of the eagles to the Land of the Great Spirit. When they landed on the far shore of Crystal Lake, they encountered chiefs, braves, and maidens who had been chained there by the Great Spirit. A breathtakingly beautiful maiden was chained with the others. The younger Seneca brave fell in love with her the moment he saw her, and he could tell from her eyes that his love was reciprocated.

The father and his two sons stayed in the Land of the Great Spirit for three days. The younger son courted the beautiful maiden and pleaded with her to come to his village to share his lodge. She told him, through her tears, that she couldn't go with him, for she was of the Land of the Great Spirit and could not return to the Earth Land. The one way that they could be together, she said, was for him to return to earth and wait for the Call of Death from the Great Spirit. Only then could they be together.

When the time came for the father and his two sons to leave for home, the younger son could not be found. They searched for him in shaded groves, in hidden valleys, and in the silvery forest. They found him lying at the base of the Tree of the Silver Arrows, which had silver shafts instead of branches and silver arrowheads in place of leaves. He had pulled one of the silver arrows from the tree and thrust it into his heart. The lovesick young brave had found a way to join his loved one in the Land of the Great Spirit.

Chapter 8

Serpents / Strange Tales

The Girl Who Was Not Satisfied with Simple Things

here was once an Iroquois maiden who was not satisfied with simple things. She rejected every suitor who expressed an interest in her. One was overweight, another didn't pay enough attention to his clothing, and a third one spoke in too coarse a manner. Her mother thought that she would never marry; no man would be good enough.

One evening at dusk a strange, handsome brave arrived at the door of their lodge. The mother invited the young warrior to enter, but he stood in the doorway and pointed at the maiden. He said, "I have come to take you as my wife." His face was radiant by the light of the fire, and he wore a wide belt of yellow and black wampum. He wore two long feathers in his headband and was graceful when he moved.

The mother asked her daughter if she would marry a stranger whose clan she didn't know after rejecting all of the suitors from her own village. The maiden made up her mind without hesitation to marry the handsome brave. She wrapped all her possessions into a bundle and followed him into the night. As she walked through the darkness, she began to be afraid. She had left the security of her mother's lodge to follow a man about whom she knew nothing.

Her husband-to-be took her by the arm, told her not to be nervous, and said that they were almost at the home of his people. She asked how that could be since they were very close to the river. He told her to follow him down the hill, and they would be home. They walked down a steep embankment to a lodge with a pair of elk horns mounted

Young Maiden and God of Thunder Overlooking Reptiles

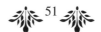

over the entranceway. He told her that she would meet his people in the morning.

The maiden heard strange noises outside of the lodge and was afraid all night. The lodge smelled of fish. She wrapped her sleeping robe tightly around her and waited anxiously for morning to come. In the morning, there was very little sunshine; the sky was hazy and overcast. The brave gave her a new dress covered with beautiful wampum. He told her that she must wear the dress to make herself ready to meet his people.

She told him that she would not wear the dress because it smelled like fish. The young warrior looked angry, but he didn't try to force her to wear the dress. He told her that he must go away for awhile, and he told her not to leave the lodge or to be afraid of anything that she saw.

The maiden began to question her rash act of coming with this young man who was a stranger to her. She missed the warmth of her mother's hearth. The young woman remembered the good, honest men from her tribe who had asked for her hand in marriage. She realized that if she had been satisfied with simple things, this would not have happened.

As she reminisced, a large horned serpent crawled in through the door. He slithered up close to her and stared into her eyes. His body was encircled by bands of yellow and black. She was terrified. Finally, he turned around and went back out through the door. She followed him to the doorway. She looked out and saw serpents everywhere. Some were crawing out of caves, and others were just lying on the rocks. Suddenly, the maiden realized that her betrothed was not what he appeared to be. He was a serpent masquerading in human form.

The maiden may have been foolish, but she had courage. She began to think of ways to escape. She decided that she would never put on the dress that the brave had asked her to wear, for that would probably turn her into a serpent. She continued to think of ways of escaping. However, she was very tired because she had gone all night without sleep. Finally, she could no longer hold her eyes open, and she slept soundly.

Her grandfather appeared to her in a dream and offered to help her out of her predicament. He told her to leave the lodge immediately and to run to the steep cliff at the edge of the village. He encouraged her not to turn back because the serpents would stop her.

When the young woman awoke, she looked out and saw her betrothed, dressed again as a handsome man, returning to the lodge. She realized that she had to act fast, or she would be trapped there forever. She dashed out of the door and headed for the cliff. The young brave called for her to return; but she ran as fast as she could for the high ground, which seemed so far away. She could hear rustling noises behind her, and the voice of the warrior calling to her to turn back.

She climbed as a driven person, using all of her strength. Her hands were scraped and bleeding, and she was very tired. As she reached the top of the cliff, she felt her grandfather reach out to help her. Then she looked back and saw many horned serpents along the shoreline and in the river below. Her grandfather, Heno the Thunderer, began to hurl bolts of lightning down on the serpents. Peals of thunder accompanied the flashes of lightning that struck and killed every one of the monsters.

The Thunderer looked down on her, and a gentle rain began to fall. She had been brave, he said, and she had helped him to get rid of the great serpents. He told her that her deed had empowered her, and that he might call upon her again for help. Then Heno raised his hand and beckoned a small cloud to come to him. He helped her onto the cloud, and it carried her back to her village.

Shortly after she returned, she married a strong, good-hearted man, and they had many children. Her grandfather visited her often, and she traveled with him to help rid the earth of evil beings. When she grew old, she advised her grandchildren, "Be satisfied with simple things."

 ## The Great Serpent and the Young Wife

young Iroquois brave married a beautiful maiden and was very much in love with her. The brave's three sisters were jealous of their sister-in-law because of her beauty, her accomplishments, and their brother's love for her. The mean-spirited sisters conceived of a plan to destroy the object of their jealousy.

It was blueberry season, and the sisters invited their brother's wife to join them in picking berries for the family. The young wife collected her baskets and climbed into a canoe to paddle across a large lake to the island where rich blueberry fields were found. She asked her sisters-in-law if she should prepare a lunch to take with them. They told her that it wasn't necessary because the blueberries were so abundant that they wouldn't be there for very long.

The four young women beached their canoe on the shore. The young wife wanted to pick berries in the fields near the canoe so that they would have to carry the berries only a short distance. The three sisters wanted to pick farther inland. They complained when their sister-in-law wouldn't come with them, but this was exactly what they wanted. They intended to leave her on the island.

The young wife worked steadily and soon had her large basket filled with the purple fruit. She slung the heavy load onto her back and fastened the burden strap—the gusha'a— around her forehead and walked back to the shore of the lake. The canoe wasn't where they had left it, and there was no sign of the three young sisters. Suddenly, she knew what they had done. She should have been more suspicious of their uncharacteristic friendliness. She sat down and cried until she was exhausted.

The young wife felt very alone and was afraid of being attacked by wild animals on the island. For all she knew, the island might contain evil creatures that could change her into a bird or an animal. She was tormented by these thoughts until dusk, when she put her head down and slept. A whooping sound over the lake awakened her. She looked out and saw flickering lights and heard the sound of many voices. The lights moved quickly from the

Young Woman Flogging Serpent with Willow Whips

water to the land and formed a circle on the shore.

The young woman hid behind a large log. She saw creatures who had some of the features of men, but who also seemed like animals, meeting in council on the beach. She realized that one of the strange beings was discussing the abandonment of the young woman on the island by her sisters-in-law. They were debating how they could help her. One member of the council pointed out that she must be removed from the island because the berries were poisoned, and, if she stayed, the singing wizard—the segoweno-ta—would bewitch her.

They asked for a volunteer to carry her across the lake to the land from which she had come. A tall creature with a deep voice offered to do it. The council chief told him that his pride exceeded his courage, and that he wouldn't be allowed to help her. A large hulk of a creature volunteered next and was told that his appearance was too terrifying, and that he would frighten the young wife. Several more beings offered their services and were told that they weren't suitable.

Finally, a tall, slender creature stood up and said in a decisive voice that he would do everything within his power to help the young woman. The council chief responded immediately, "You are the chosen one. You are close to the people!" The council adjourned and the flickering lights reappeared over the lake. The young wife crawled back to the place where she had slept the previous evening. She was very apprehensive as she lay her head down and tried to sleep.

Just before dawn, the young woman heard a voice calling to her from the lake. She ran to the shore and saw what appeared to be a huge canoe in the water. She looked closely and identified it as a large serpent with curved horns on his proud head. He told her that he had come to rescue her, and that she should sit upon his head and hold onto his horns. He told her to first break twelve rods from a willow tree to use as whips if he slowed down on their journey.

The young wife climbed up upon the serpent's head and placed the twelve willow whips in her lap. The serpent began to move through the water in a smooth, undulating motion. The girl was far enough above the surface of the water to stay dry. He told her that he was a member of a race of underwater people who were hated by Heno, the Thunder Spirit. The serpent told her that if Heno's scouts, the small black clouds, spotted them, the Thunder Spirit would send thunder clouds after them.

The serpent had just told her this, when they saw a small black cloud moving toward them and felt the wind begin to blow. The serpent told his passenger to whip him so that they might stay ahead of Heno's warriors. She whipped him hard until most of her willow rods were broken. Dark clouds scudded across the sky, and they heard loud peals of thunder in the distance. The serpent was moving through the water so fast that he was creating foam. The claps of thunder grew louder as the Thunder Spirit came closer.

Heno threw a bolt of lightning that struck a floating oak log near them. The sound of thunder was earsplitting. Many bolts of lightning, which looked like sheets of fire, lit up the lake and the shoreline in the distance. The serpent knew that the race would be close, so he appealed to the young wife to whip him hard with her remaining willow rods. He knew that his strength was failing, but he planned to do everything that he could to get her to the shore. He asked her to burn tobacco in his memory on the lakeshore twice a year if he got her there safely.

A bolt of lightning struck the water next to them, and the serpent told her to jump off because he was going to dive. The young wife was sad that they had come so close to safety, but had failed. The serpent plunged below the surface of the lake and disappeared. The black clouds began to disburse, the storm diminished, and the sun broke through the few remaining clouds. As she swam, her high regard for her rescuer left her when she considered that he had abandoned her just before victory was theirs.

She was too tired to swim any longer, and she began to sink. She was astonished to find sand beneath her feet. She waded out of the lake and rested, exhausted and frightened, at the base of a tree. The storm moved on from the area, grumbling that it had failed to kill Djodikwado, the serpent. After resting, she stood up and looked around, filled with gratitude for her deliverer.

She saw a man with a drooping head, who appeared to be wandering aimlessly in a melancholy state. He had been soaked by the rain and looked by his entire demeanor to be very dispirited. She

 57

called out to him, "Husband, oh husband, is it truly you?" He turned to her and exclaimed, "Wife, oh wife, returned living, is it you?"

As they walked, arm in arm, to the lodge, the wife explained to her husband what his sisters had done. The three sisters were surprised to see their sister-in-law. The husband banished his sisters from their home forever. The couple lived a long and happy life in which envy and jealousy had no place.

Hiawatha's Taming of Ododarhoh

iawatha, the peace-loving Onondaga chief, counseled for friendship among the nations at a time when retribution was a way of life. If an Iroquois were killed, the victim's male relatives would kill the murderer. If the murderer couldn't be located, one of his relatives would be killed in his place. Revenge was a way of life; it didn't matter if innocent people lost their lives.

An evil character named Ododarhoh lived south of the main Onondaga village. He lived alone in a dark ravine near a marsh and slept on a bed of bullrushes. According to legend, the long, intertwined locks of his hair were living snakes. He was a wizard feared by the nearby Onondagas and was a cannibal who ate men, women, and children raw. Ododarhoh committed the unspeakable crime of killing Hiawatha's wife and seven daughters (three daughters in some versions of the story).

When Hiawatha learned of their deaths, he threw himself to the ground and thrashed around in self-torture. His grief was so deep that people hesitated to approach him to offer their consolation. He left the village, built a lodge of hemlock branches, and became a hermit and an aimless wanderer. Hiawatha was expected to kill Ododarhoh, but it wasn't his nature to commit an act of revenge that wouldn't bring back his wife and daughters.

When Hiawatha was in the depths of his grief, he was visited at his lodge by Degandawida the Peacemaker. Degandawida was a Huron evangelist who was attempting to convince the Iroquois

Confederation to stop fighting among themselves and to live in peace. He wasn't having much success because he was an outsider and because he stuttered. He sought the help of Hiawatha, who was respected within the confederation and was an outstanding speaker.

Hiawatha immediately became a follower of Degandawida; it was too late to save his own family, but perhaps he could work with the Peacemaker to save the lives of others. Degandawida's ideas brought Hiawatha out of his grief.

The Peacemaker wanted to convince the Onondagas and the other nations of the confederacy to implement the plans for peace that he and Hiawatha were proposing from village to village. His plan was to convert Ododarhoh from his evil ways and to use Hiawatha as the instrument of this conversion. If the Onondagas saw that Hiawatha, upon whom Ododarhoh had inflicted such a terrible injustice, could forgive his tormenter and convince him to follow the path of peace, then the rest of the nation would follow.

Degandawida and Hiawatha visited the evil wizard at his lodge in the dark ravine, where Hiawatha pacified Ododarhoh by singing to him and speaking the message of peace and of Iroquois unity. Ododarhoh's two visitors expected him to react violently, because they knew of his opposition to peace and unity. They expected to be attacked, but Ododarhoh raised his head and said that he would mend his ways and abide by these proposals of peace and unity. Hiawatha then combed the snakes, which symbolized evil and insane thoughts, out of the wizard's hair. Thus Hiawatha (Ayonwartha) was given his name, which meant "He Who Combs."

The Onondaga Nation followed Ododarhoh into the Iroquois Confederation and the Great Peace. An Onondaga village near Syracuse became the capital of the confederation and the location of the council fire. Ododarhoh was named "firekeeper," a position comparable to president of the senate. He became one of the most powerful of the sachems.

Ithaca's Dr. Jekyll and Mr. Hyde

dward Rulloff was born Edward H. Rulloffson near St. John's, New Brunswick, Canada, on July 9, 1820. As a young man he worked as a clerk in a store. After he was caught stealing by the proprietor, he served two years in jail. He moved to Ithaca in 1842 to make a fresh start in life. Although he had little formal education, he was intelligent and believed in self-education. He became a school teacher in Dryden. One of his pupils was Harriet Schutt, the daughter of a prominent local farmer. Harriet fell in love with her teacher, and they were married on December 31, 1843.

Rulloff left his teaching job and worked for a druggist in Ithaca, where he picked up some knowledge of medicine. In 1844, the Rulloffs moved to Lansing near Rogues' Harbor, where he had cards printed "Doct. Edward H. Rulloff" and began to practice as a doctor. In early 1845, a daughter was born to the Rulloffs. Edward and Harriet were often heard quarreling, and he was very jealous of her. The neighbors knew that Rulloff treated his wife cruelly.

June 23, 1845, was the last day that Harriet and her three-month-old baby daughter were seen alive. Olive Robertson, who lived across the road with her parents, Mr. and Mrs. Thomas Robertson, testified later that both the mother and child appeared to be in good health. On the next morning, Mrs. Robertson observed that, for the first time, the shutters had been closed on the Rulloff's house.

At noon, Rulloff visited his neighbors to borrow a horse and wagon from Thomas Robertson. Rulloff told Robertson that he was returning a chest that he had borrowed from one of Harriet's relatives. Robertson helped him load the chest into the wagon and noted that his end of the chest weighed about sixty to seventy pounds. Rulloff also loaded a large sack that was about one-third full into the wagon. Later, Harriet's relative said that he had not loaned a chest to Rulloff and had not received one from him.

Rulloff told his neighbors that Harriet and their daughter were visiting relatives in Madison, Ohio. He mentioned that they might be back in two or three weeks, or that they might not return. Then he traveled to Geneva, Rochester, Buffalo, and to Cleveland. Harriet's brother, Ephraim Schutt, followed Rulloff and caught up with him on a westbound train in Rochester. Rulloff promised to accompany him to visit the Schutt relatives where Harriet and their daughter were supposedly staying. However, Rulloff slipped away from Ephraim in Buffalo.

Ephraim continued on to Madison, Ohio, where he found no trace of his sister and niece. Upon his return to Cleveland he saw Rulloff, who now claimed that his wife and daughter were missing. He said that he didn't know where they were. Rulloff returned to Ithaca where an alarmed populace insisted that he be prosecuted. Cayuga Lake was

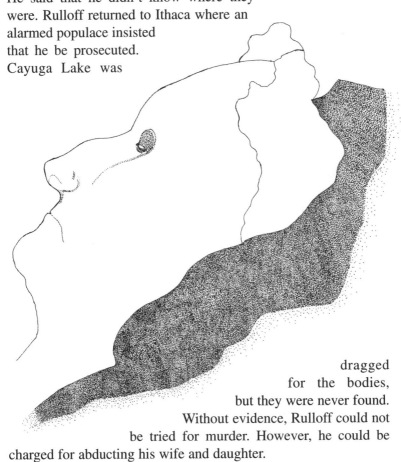

dragged for the bodies, but they were never found. Without evidence, Rulloff could not be tried for murder. However, he could be charged for abducting his wife and daughter.

Rulloff was found guilty of abduction in Tompkins County

Court and was sentenced to ten years in the Auburn State Prison. He took advantage of his time in prison to develop a proficiency in languages. He had books, time, and the motivation to learn. On his release from prison after having served his sentence, he was arrested again for the murder of his wife and family. He went to court a second time and was held in jail in Ithaca while awaiting the verdict.

While the court of appeals was considering his case, Rulloff escaped from the Ithaca jail with the help of Albert Jarvis, the jailer's son. Jarvis drove a carriage pulled by a team of black horses to the door of the jail, and Rulloff took the reins and headed down the road to Elmira. The carriage and horses were found abandoned the next day. The cold weather on the night of his escape caused him to lose two toes to frostbite.

Rulloff moved to western Pennsylvania, where he impressed the president of a small college with his knowledge of languages and was offered a professorship. However, he couldn't change from his criminal ways. He robbed a jewelry store and had the misfortune to be identified by a fellow inmate from Auburn, who had returned to live in Pennsylvania. Rulloff was returned to Ithaca to await the verdict in his appeal. The court of appeals overturned the lower court's decision because the bodies still had not been found.

The people of Tompkins County were not pleased that Rulloff was going to get away unpunished. A poster with the question, "Shall the murderer go unpunished?", was widely distributed. On Saturday, March 12, 1859, a meeting was held at Clinton House in Ithaca to decide Rulloff's fate. Citizens were ready to take the law into their own hands. A huge battering ram the size of a telegraph pole was hidden in Six Mile Creek to use if Sheriff Robertson refused to release the prisoner. Construction of a gallows was begun.

Sheriff Robertson was determined to protect his prisoner from being lynched. On the morning of March 11 a carriage pulled up to the jail, and the sheriff got in and drove off alone. When the citizens assigned to watch the jail went to breakfast, Robertson returned and spirited his prisoner away to the steamboat dock. A Cayuga Lake steamer was preparing to leave the dock, and the sheriff and Rulloff jumped aboard and were on their way to Auburn and the safety of the state prison. The crowd of 5,000 citizens who were prepared to storm the Ithaca jail were irate. They were still mad at the time of the next election, when they voted Sheriff Robertson out of office.

Rulloff lived in New York City for several years, where he spent considerable time in the New York Public Library. He continued to study languages and eventually was fluent in French, German, Greek, Italian, and Latin and had some knowledge of Hebrew and Sanskrit. He wrote a manuscript entitled "Method in the Formation of Language," in which he attempted to show the common origin of all languages. As Professor Edouard Leurio, Rulloff presented his manuscript at a conference of the American Philological Association at Vassar College in Poughkeepsie in 1867.

Rulloff continued to alternate between constructive activity and criminal activity. He was jailed several times in New York, usually for burglary, and he served some time in Sing Sing prison in Ossining. He excelled at being an imposter; his early effort to pose as a medical doctor was just the beginning.

In New Hampshire, Rulloff masqueraded as an Episcopal clergyman and a graduate of Oxford University. That ruse lasted until a local store was burglarized, and the stolen items were found in Rulloff's possession. He was sentenced to ten years in prison, but he escaped after serving just three months.

In 1869, Rulloff returned to the Finger Lakes Region. In Cortland he posed as an attorney and represented a man, Dexter, who was indicted for burglary. Rulloff decided that he might as well use the knowledge of the law that he had accumulated sitting in a courtroom as an indicted person.

The beginning of the end for Rulloff came on August 17, 1870, when he, his client, Dexter, and Albert Jarvis, who had helped him to escape from jail in Ithaca, attempted to rob the Halbert and Brothers dry goods store in Binghamton. The intruders startled two clerks who were sleeping in their quarters over the store. Rulloff shot and killed one of the clerks with his pistol and wounded the other. The burglars fled toward the Chenango River, while the wounded clerk sounded the alarm. The next morning a widespread manhunt was begun. The bodies of Dexter and Jarvis were found

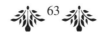

floating in the Chenango River. Suspicious bruises were found on their bodies.

Rulloff was captured while walking along the railroad tracks leading out of Binghamton. The surviving clerk from the store could not identify Rulloff because he didn't get a good look at him. However, the burglars had left behind their tools and a pair of shoes. The shoes had an indentation over the wearer's missing toes. Since Rulloff had had two frostbitten toes amputated after his escape from jail in Ithaca, the shoes were used to prove his presence in the store.

Rulloff's trial was held in Binghamton in January, 1871. He admitted nothing, but it took the jury only six hours to reach a verdict of guilty. Rulloff was sentenced to be hanged on March 3. The date was postponed due to an appeal, and the hanging was rescheduled for May 18. Rulloff persisted in claiming that he was innocent. He blamed the murder of the clerk on one of his accomplices who had been found floating in the river. By this time, however, Rulloff's credibility with the public and the press was nonexistent.

In writing about Rulloff, one newsman observed, "He is a man entirely devoid of the finer sensibilities of human nature, brutish and crime-hardened to the last degree possible, and incapable of appreciating or comprehending the motives that prompt the press to sustain law and order."

Rulloff was five feet, nine inches tall and weighed about 175 pounds. He had dark eyes, black hair, and a beard with a trace of gray. Rulloff's head was large for a man his size, and he had small, almost feminine hands. It is difficult to believe that Rulloff could have deceived so many people during his lifetime. However, he was a captivating conversationalist, and he had a dominating personality. When he was excited, his eyes sparkled.

A number of famous people, including Horace Greeley of the New York *Tribune*, were impressed by Rulloff and asked the governor to pardon him. Mark Twain also thought that Rulloff's life should be spared. Twain wrote a letter to the New York *Tribune* noting that Rulloff had contributions to make to society, and that his death would be society's loss. He wrote:

For it is plain that in the person of Rulloff one of the most

marvelous intellects that any age has produced is about to be sacrificed, and that, too, while half of the mystery of its strange powers is yet a secret. Here is a man who has never entered the doors of a college or a university, and yet, by the sheer might of his innate gifts has made himself such a colossus in abstruse learning that the ablest of our scholars are but pygmies in his presence....

Every learned man who enters Rulloff's presence leaves it amazed and confounded by his prodigious capabilities and attainments. One scholar said he did not believe that in the matters of subtle analysis, vast knowledge in his peculiar field of research, comprehensive grasp of subject and serene kingship over its limitless and bewildering details, any land or any era of modern times had given birth to Rulloff's equal.

On May 18, 1871, a large crowd attended the hanging of Edward H. Rulloff in Binghamton. Governor John T. Hoffman had rejected all pleas for a pardon.

Rulloff's brain was removed in an autopsy and preserved in Dr. Wilder's collection in Stimson Hall, Cornell University. It weighed seven ounces more than the average brain, was heavier than that of William Thackeray, and weighed five ounces more than Daniel Webster's brain. Many reminders of the life of Edward Rulloff are on display at the DeWitt Historical Society in Ithaca. One of the most eye-catching items in their collection is Rulloff's death mask, which was created by an Ithaca artist.

Edward Rulloff continues to be one the more controversial personalities from the Finger Lakes Region. Unfortunately, he wasted his talent. By pursuing a life of crime, he missed the opportunity of making significant contributions to society.

 ## Olde Germania's Ghost

n December 17, 1994, Olde Germania Wine Cellars opened at 8299 Pleasant Valley Road, Hammondsport, on the site of Germania Wine Cellars. Germania Wine Cellars had been founded by Jacob Frey, a Swiss immigrant, in 1870. The winery won many medals, including an award at the Paris Exposition in 1900. Subsequently, Germania Wine Cellars became a part of the Taylor Wine Company.

Jim Gifford headed the group of investors that purchased Germania Wine Cellars and is restoring it. Gifford, who majored in food science and oenology at Fresno State, began his winemaking career at the Gold Seal Winery, then owned by Joseph Seagram & Son, in 1980. When Seagram closed Gold Seal, Gifford continued working for them in a joint venture with the French champagne house, G. H. Mumm, in Napa Valley, California. In 1987, Jim left Seagram to become the winemaker for Glenora Winery on Seneca Lake. In 1989, he became a wine industry consultant.

The Olde Germania Wine Cellars complex consists of nine buildings, all built before 1903, including the historic four-story main building. Above the winetasting area in the main building is the Great Western Hall of Fame, where the Pleasant Valley Wine Company held their marketing meetings. The walls are lined with portraits of Pleasant Valley Wine Company officers and marketing managers. The room has remained intact, with the exception of a large oak table that has been removed. The main building, with its rough-sawn planks, still houses the original ageing tanks and wine barrels. Three of the barrels came to the United States on a sailing vessel in 1858.

Many old buildings have ghost stories associated with them, and this winery is no exception. Evidence of the ghost of Olde Germania has occurred on numerous occasions. Once Gifford and his son were using a hose connected to a spigot in the cellar of the main building. When they checked to see why the water had stopped flowing, they found that the spigot had been turned off. No one else was in the building, and neither Gifford nor his son had

"Stubby" the Ghost at Olde Germania Winery

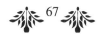

turned off the spigot. On another occasion, a wine pump was turned to a higher speed even though no one had been anywhere near it.

As a result of these ghost stories, a former Great Western foreman told Jim that he couldn't get anyone to work at night in the cellar, which housed Great Western's Solera Sherry operation, and that some of the employees wouldn't work alone in the cellar during the day. The carpenter / woodworker who did much of the restoration heard a strange voice while working alone. Some residents believe that the ghost of Clarence "Stubby" Taylor haunts the building, and that the ghost is the source of the mysterious activities and the voice. Clarence W. Taylor was the second oldest son of Walter and Addie Taylor, the founders of the Taylor Wine Company.

The buildings of Olde Germania Wine Cellars were vacant for a number of years. Apparently "Stubby" is equally at home whether the buildings are occupied or not. He certainly has chosen a historic site located in a beautiful valley for his residence.

 ## The Pompey Stone Hoax

he Finger Lakes Region has always been known for hoaxes, particularly in the hills around Ithaca and Syracuse. The best known are the Cardiff Giant, discovered south of Syracuse in 1869, and the Taughannock Giant, unearthed near Trumansburg in 1879. The hoax of the Pompey Stone predates those two hoaxes by fifty to sixty years.

In the summer of 1820, Philo Cleveland uncovered an oval-shaped boulder on his farm south of Syracuse, while clearing a field. As he pried the boulder out of the ground with his crowbar, he thought that he could see lettering on its underside. However, he simply moved the boulder, which was twelve inches wide, fourteen inches long, and eight inches thick, onto a pile with the other

The Pompey Stone

stones. He thought little about it until he walked by it several days later after a rain had washed away the dirt that had obscured lettering on the stone.

The boulder had been inscribed with the following lettters and numbers:

Leo X De   L. S.

VI 1520-   + fl

A fine, roughhewn line had been inscribed between the De and the L. and the S. Cleveland lifted the boulder into his wagon and transported it to Cy Avery's blacksmith shop at Oran, where it was the subject of much speculation.

The boulder was taken to the museum of the Albany Institute for evaluation by its archaeologists. In their opinion, the inscription could be interpreted as, "Leo X by the grace of God, sixth year of his Pontificate, 1520." This interpretation was supported by the

fact that Leo X was elected Pope in 1514. They thought that the boulder was a headstone, and that the L. and S. were the initials of the deceased. Furthermore, they stated that the cross under the letters L. and S. indicated that he was a Roman Catholic and that the inverted U meant that he was a member of the Masonic Order. They speculated that the deceased had been a native of Spain.

One scholar conjectured that, "Possibly, some adventurer of this nation, allured by the story of a lake at the north whose bottom was lined with silver [the salt at Salina Springs] traversed the region in pursuit of the darling object ... the survivor or survivors may have placed this monument over his remains." Henry Rowe Schoolcraft, an ethnologist and geologist, observed that Florida was discovered by Ponce de Leon in 1512 and speculated that a band of his men may have traveled north to Philo Cleveland's farm. He added, "As a mere historical question a claim to the discovery of the interior of New York by the Spanish crown might in this view find something to base itself on."

In 1879, Henry A. Holmes, librarian of the New York State Library, speculated before the Oneida Historical Society that the boulder was a sepulchral monument to a European, probably a Spaniard. Furthermore, the European may have been captured by the Iroquois, adopted into a tribe, and attained the status of sachem. However, a pall was cast over all of this conjecture by the state archaeologist, Dr. William M. Beauchamp, a savvy scientist. He observed that the letters and numbers on the boulder were of recent origin and that the marks on the stone had been made by two cold chisels "of good quality," a hammer, and a smith's punch that he thought "would make a pretty good kit of tools for a wandering Spaniard."

This statement cast considerable doubt on the authenticity of the boulder. However, a letter written in 1894 by John E. Sweet, an upstanding citizen of Syracuse, ended all speculation about the authenticity of the stone:

> My uncle Cyrus Avery, born in Pompey, lived there during the early part of the century, and told me the last time I saw him, in 1867, that he and his nephew William Willard of this city cut the figures on the Pompey Stone just to see

what would come of it. When the account appeared in
Clark's history, so much had come of it that they decided
it was best to keep still altogether.... The tools were exactly the ones most likely to be at hand in Grandfather
Avery's blacksmith shop at Oran....

Mr. Avery was given to just that sort of thing. The Pompey
Stone is nothing more or less than a joke. It can hardly be
called a fraud, as it does not pretend to be anything, nor did
the makers do anything to make it appear that it was.
Really I hardly think the stone worth sending back to
Albany, and Mr. Beauchamp may congratulate himself
upon having sized up the inscription so accurately.

(Signed) John E. Sweet, June 11, 1894

Chapter 9

Travails / Tragedies

The Burning of the *Frontenac* on Cayuga Lake

efore automobiles and trucks began to appear on the few horse-drawn carriage and wagon roads early in the twentieth century, steamboats were a principal means of transportation on the Finger Lakes. Steamboats were a particularly important method of travel on Cayuga Lake, which, at forty miles long, is the longest Finger Lake.

In 1819, the Cayuga Steamboat Company was formed to provide transportation for passengers and cargo on the lake. The company launched three steamboats during the 1820s: *Enterprise* in 1820, *Telemachus* in 1827, and *Dewitt Clinton* in 1829. Timothy Dwight (T. D.)Wilcox owned and operated one of the larger passenger boat companies on Cayuga Lake. His boats, of which he purchased some and had others built for him, included the *Aurora*, the *Beardsley*, the *Cayuga*, the *Forest City*, the *Howland*, the *Ithaca*, the *Kate Morgan*, the *Sheldrake*, and the *Simeon DeWitt*.

Wilcox's largest steamboat was the *Frontenac*, the flagship of his fleet. The *Frontenac,* which was 135 feet long with a beam of twenty-two feet, was built in 1870 at a cost of $50,000. She was a side-wheeler propelled by two 27-horsepower engines at a maximum speed of 15 knots. The *Frontenac* had a large dining room and provided cabins for 350 passengers. Apparently, the steamboat was named for Frontenac Island, which is located off the eastern shore of Cayuga Lake near Union Springs. Frontenac Island, in turn, was named for one of the early French governors of colonial Canada, the Comte de Frontenac.

Wilcox's passenger line was a highly successful business. In 1888, four years after his death, his heirs sold the company to the Cayuga Lake Transportation Company. They operated the business until 1902, when they sold it to Captain Melvin T. Brown of Syracuse. Brown, an experienced steamship captain, had operated the *Jacob Amos* on Onondaga Lake for thirty years. When he bought the business, Brown had the superstructure of the *Frontenac* rebuilt and, in 1907, had the boilers replaced at a cost of $5,000.

According to its schedule, the *Frontenac* left the dock in Ithaca at 9:00 a.m., made about a dozen stops en route to the village of Cayuga on the eastern shore near the northern end of the lake, and began the return trip to Ithaca at 1:15 p.m. In 1907, the round-trip cost $1.00. Occasionally, the schedule would be changed to accommodate excursions.

On July, 26, 1907, a special excursion caused the *Frontenac* to stay overnight at Cayuga, and the passengers who wanted to return to Ithaca that Friday afternoon boarded the *Mohawk* for the return trip. On Saturday morning the *Frontenac* left Cayuga with the passengers who had originally been scheduled to return to Ithaca on the *Mohawk*. The *Frontenac* and the *Mohawk* met at Sheldrake at 11:00 a.m. on Saturday to allow both boats to assume their normal schedules. The passengers going north boarded the *Frontenac*, and the passengers going south boarded the *Mohawk*, which returned to Ithaca.

Two of the young women who went aboard the *Frontenac* at Sheldrake were Marietta Sullivan, a vacationing stenographer with a Syracuse law firm, and Lida Bennett of Frankfort, who had just completed a three-week course at the Prang School of Art at Glenwood. Eight other women who had attended the course at Glenwood also went aboard the *Frontenac* at Sheldrake.

The passenger list included the wife of John Genung, the sheriff of Tompkins County, and their nine-year-old son, Roland; Mrs. Lena Genung, wife of Dr. Homer Genung of Freeville, and their four-year-old son, Karl; and Stella Clinton, a manager in an Ithaca department store.

Three Cornell University summer students also boarded the *Frontenac* at Sheldrake: Zalia McCreary of Cohoes, Eliza Tuttle of Middletown, and Eva Mott of Port Allegany, Pennsylvania. Also

boarding were Mrs. Etta Clark of Seneca Falls and Mrs. John Abel and her daughter and granddaughter. When the *Frontenac* left Sheldrake, she carried approximately sixty passengers—eight or nine men and the rest women and children. They were scheduled to pick up forty additional passengers at Aurora.

Captain Brown and crew of six were aboard that day, including the pilot, engineer, fireman, stewardess, and two deck hands. Captain Brown's wife and their grandson were also on board. Mrs. Brown helped with the food preparation and service.

The *Frontenac* crossed the lake in fifty-mile-per-hour winds from the northwest that caused waves that were six feet high. The steamboat was unable to dock at either Aurora or Levanna, which were the next two scheduled stops. The boat steamed north to Farley's Point, where a number of cottages lined the shore. The Ithaca *Daily News* reported that: "James Ferris ... was seated on the porch of his cottage waiting for the boat. It was to make a landing at the dock at Farley's, and in heavy weather he thought there would be considerable trouble. He said it was just one o'clock when he saw the boat. 'There she comes,' he said, and then saw smoke and flames. He cried out, 'My God, she's on fire!'"

Ferris ran for help. Most of the passengers were below deck out of the wind, and no one on the *Frontenac* had yet seen the smoke and flames. People on the dock called out to the crew and passengers to attract their attention. Nine-year-old Roland Genung and his mother were sitting on deck chairs on the upper deck when the young man saw smoke coming from the pilot house. Mrs. Genung thought it was steam or smoke from cooking until she saw the flames.

Roland ran below to warn Captain Brown. Brown ordered the engineer to start the pumps and ran to the upper deck and trained the fire hose onto the fire. However, the fire had gotten a good start and was being fanned by the high winds. When he saw that he was not gaining on the fire, Brown ran to the pilot house and ordered pilot Smith to beach the steamboat. Then the captain ran back and manned the fire hose until he realized that the fire was out of control.

Brown removed life preservers from their racks and threw the life jackets down the ladder to the second deck. When the

Frontenac beached, most of the passengers gathered in the bow. The water was about four feet deep just off the bow. Both the captain and his wife helped the women and children put on life preservers. The Captain's wife and their grandson jumped off the bow into shallow water. The heat within twenty-five feet of the boat was so intense that those in the water had to continually duck their heads under the surface to cool off.

Mrs. Clark jumped into the water and felt herself being pushed toward the boat by wave action. She kicked and paddled toward shore until she found herself underwater. Mr. Murphy, an Ithaca tailor staying at one of the cottages, pulled Mrs. Clark's head up out of the water and guided her toward the shore. Murphy helped many people survive that day.

The lifeboats caught fire and were of no use to the struggling crew and passengers. Obviously, those who could swim were at a decided advantage over those who could not. Miss Lois Reidel of Utica, who had attended the art session at Glenwood, was one of the strong swimmers; she helped many passengers reach the shore. The *Frontenac* continued to burn rapidly. Those who were burned cried out in pain.

Unfortunately, the eight or nine male passengers did not do much to assist the women and children. The Ithaca *Daily Journal* quoted Captain Brown, "Had the eight or nine men passengers on the boat not displayed the worst cowardice I have ever seen in all my experiences on the lake, I doubt if a single life would have been lost on Saturday."

Mrs. Clark was quoted in the Utica *Herald-Dispatch*, "I saw Mr. Murphy save many other people, doing noble work every moment. I tell you many of the passengers owe their lives to that man. He said to me, 'It makes me sick to see those men coming ashore in life preservers instead of standing by the boat to get the women away and started for the shore.' Those men did nothing but save themselves."

Another good Samaritan was the Reverend A. A. McKay of Auburn who was camping nearby in a tent with seven boys from his congregation. He helped many people get ashore. Other heroes were Hart Carr of Union Springs and Mr. and Mrs. Jacob Dill, who lived on a farm in the area.

By 1:30 p.m., the shore was lined with seven bodies, five women and two children, for whom valiant attempts to administer artificial respiration had failed. The children were six-year-old Grace Abel and four-year-old Karl Genung. Among the women were Stella Clinton, who returned to the burning boat for her suitcase, and Zalia McCreary, a Cornell summer student who drowned after losing her grip on a life float when a wave broke over her.

Lida Bennett, who had attended the session at Glenwood, died of exposure. Another victim was Syracuse resident Marietta Sullivan, who was afraid to jump and sank under the waves as soon as she entered the water. Eva Mott, another Cornell summer student, was not identified until a response was received to a description of her in the Auburn *Daily Advertiser*.

The source of the fire was never determined, but it is clear that the wind-whipped fire went out of control almost as soon as it started. Captain Brown and his crew were exonerated of any negligence in the disaster. The question was raised as to why the boat's whistle, which could be heard for six miles, was not used to warn people below decks of the fire and to call for help from shore.

The Brown Transportation Company temporarily replaced the *Frontenac* with the *Comanche*, and $50,000 was set aside to build a permanent replacement at an Ithaca boatyard during the following winter. Despite the disaster, the volume of steamboat passenger traffic on Cayuga Lake was not diminished.

The Destruction of the Portageville Railroad Bridge

wooden railroad bridge was constructed in 1851-52 at a narrow point across the Genesee River gorge, near the Upper Falls, in what is now Letchworth State Park. The bridge was built on thirteen 30-foot-high stone pillars, and 246 acres of timber were used. It was over 800 feet long with 190-foot-high trestles and 14-foot-high trusses; it stood 234 feet above the river bed, including the height of the stone pillars. It was constructed so that any part could be removed and repaired or replaced without weakening the structure.

The dedication ceremony, attended by Governor Hunt and President Loder and other officials of the Erie Railroad, was held on August 25, 1852. Guards were posted on the bridge around the clock to protect it from arsonists and vandals.

Early in the morning of May 6, 1875, one of the guards discovered a fire at the western end of the bridge and attempted to use a fire hose to put it out. He was unable to turn on the valve. The spectacular fire lit up the entire area, and, at 4:15 a.m., the superstructure of the western end of the bridge sank into the gorge with a loud roar.

The Erie Railroad replaced the wooden bridge with one made of 1,300,000 pounds of iron. Alternate stone pillars were removed, and the new bridge was built on the remaining pillars topped by four square feet of additional stone and capped with cast iron plates. The new bridge, 817 feet long and 255 feet high, was built on independent spans; the collapse of one span would not affect the other spans. Allowance for expansion and contraction was provided by steel rollers placed on a bedplate at the western end of the bridge. The first train crossed the new bridge on July 31, 1875.

In 1903, 260 tons of iron were replaced by an equal weight of steel. The Portage Railroad Bridge, billed as a "wonder of the world" when it was built, is still an impressive sight today. One of the best views of the bridge is from the Glen Iris Inn.

 ## The "Lost" Town of Williamsburg

The town of Williamsburg was conceived in 1792 by the agent for the Pulteney Estates and pioneer developer of the Finger Lakes Region, Charles Williamson. He envisioned Williamsburg as the commercial center of the burgeoning Genesee Country. It was the first settlement in Livingston County and the site of the first agricultural fair in Upstate New York. It was located three miles south of Geneseo, at the confluence of Canaseraga Creek and the Genesee River.

Williamson, an early developer of commerce and transportation in the region, was called "the Father of Western New York." He founded Bath and Sodus Point and assisted with the development of Geneva and Lyons, but Williamsburg was his first settlement. When he came to the site in the summer of 1792, the Wadsworth brothers had been living in their log cabin at Big Tree (Geneseo) for two years. Rochester did not yet exist but Indian Allen was operating a grist mill on the Genesee River where Rochester would emerge. The main population centers in the expanding Finger Lakes Region were Canandaigua and Geneva. In the summer of 1792, less than 1,000 settlers lived in the region west of Geneva.

Williamson delegated the task of building the town of Williamsburg, which was named for Sir William Pulteney, to John Johnstone. By the fall of 1792, Johnstone had constructed a town square including a farmhouse, a grist mill, a row of cabins, a general store, a tavern, and a large L-shaped "long barn" for Williamson's use.

The English syndicate headed by Lord Pulteney established a six-year share crop plan to develop Williamsburg. They commissioned a peddler, William Berczy, to recruit German farm workers to settle the town. However, instead of recruiting farm workers, Berczy signed up sixty immigrants from the slums of Hamburg. Only thirty of them made their way to Williamsburg to become the town's first settlers. Their unsuitability for the harsh frontier life was immediately obvious. They were unskilled in the use of axes and saws, and their work ethic left much to be desired.

The settlement was in difficulty from the beginning. Berczy claimed that the syndicate had not provided as much housing as they had promised and had not given the settlers the plows, spinning wheels, and tools that were specifed in the contract with the immigrants. Berczy began to accumulate debts, and considerable dissent existed within the community. Finally, after finding errors in Berczy's accounts and realizing that the Germans were not going to till the soil, Williamson fired Berczy.

When Williamson told the immigrants that no land was going to be transferred to them, they attacked him; he was lucky to escape injury. Williamson appealed to the frontier court, and a sheriff's posse escorted the German troublemakers to jail in Canandaigua. This ended the attempt to establish a German settlement in Genesee Country.

The development of the town was continued by settlers from New England and Pennsylvania and a few of Williamson's fellow Scotsmen. Williamson built a ball room, a blacksmith's shop, a community center, and a distillery, and he expanded the tavern. In the fall of 1793, Williamson promoted "the Williamsburg Fair and Races at the Great Forks of the Genesee for the sale of cattle, horses, and sheep." The event featured games, horse racing on a track on the flats, an ox roast, and wrestling with the Native Americans. The Fair and Races were successful and were held again in 1794. In 1795, the event was shifted to Bath, which was Williamson's headquarters and the location of his principal residence.

Williamsburg reached its peak in 1795-96. During those years, the town had forty houses, and a dry goods store and a warehouse were constructed. However, trouble was on the horizon. Williamson had spent large sums of money to promote the region. According to one account, he had spent $1,000,000 to promote a region that only provided $1,000 a month in revenues. He had built hotels, roads, and schools, and had established the region's first newspaper and theater.

In 1801, Williamson was dismissed as the land agent for the Pulteney syndicate and was replaced by a more conservative agent, Robert Troup. Williamsburg's death knell was sounded with the dismissal of its founder. Troup had no attachment for Williamsburg and was not optimistic about its future. Settlers began to move from the settlement, and Geneseo became the more favored place to live. In 1821, Geneseo was chosen over Williamsburg as the county seat of Livingston County.

Today, no sign remains of the settlement at Williamsburg other than a cemetery on a hill nearby. Two of Rochester's founders, Charles Carroll and William Fitzhugh, are buried in the cemetery. Williamson died of yellow fever in 1806 while traveling to the West Indies and was buried at sea. Local historian Arch Merrill wrote in *The White Woman and Her Valley:*

And they say—and of course it is sheer fantasy—that on soft moonlit nights a tall figure astride a noble chestnut horse comes galloping down the Valley road like the wind. The spectral rider wears a blue cloak and a tricorn hat. He reins his steed where the waters of the Genesee and the Canaseraga unite. It is Charles Williamson, the land agent, looking for his City of the Genesee.

Mr. Eastman's Disloyal Employee

George Eastman, the founder of the photographic industry, first became interested in photography in 1869. His interest intensified in the summer of 1877, when he purchased almost $100 worth of "sundries and lenses," and arranged for a local photographer to teach him "the art of photography." Taking photographs in 1877 was a complex process requiring much equipment. The glass plates had to be exposed in the camera while wet, and development had to be completed before the emulsion dried. Eastman was bothered by the cumbersomeness of the process. He commented, "... the bulk of the paraphernalia worried me. It seemed that one ought to be able to carry less than a pack-horse load." Initially, he concentrated on inventing photographic dry plates.

Eastman used Dr. Samuel Lattimore, head of the department of chemistry at the University of Rochester, as a consultant. The first chemist hired by Eastman was Henry Reichenbach, one of Dr. Lattimore's assistants. Eastman became too involved with the operation of the business to devote much time to experiments; however, he continued to work on mechanical developments, such as roller mechanisms. A patent for manufacturing transparent nitro-cellulose photographic film in rolls was granted to Reichenbach on December 10, 1889. Joint patents were granted to Eastman and Reichenbach on March 22, 1892, and July 19, 1892.

Early in the life of his company, Eastman faced one challenge that he least expected—employee disloyalty. Reichenbach and two other employees secretly formed a rival company using the film-making formulae and processes of the Eastman company. Eastman found that the three men had also made 39,400 feet of unusable film and had let 1,417 gallons of emulsion spoil while they were working for him. Eastman discharged them. It is easy to forget, when viewing a successful enterprise, that the organization evolved through a series of challenges, successes, and resolutions of short-term failures.

 ## Mr. Eastman's First Product Recall

George Eastman's early thinking about photo-graphic emulsions was given direction by an article in the *British Journal of Photography* that provided a for-mula for a sensitive gelatine emulsion for glass plates that could be used when dry. He spent long hours experimenting until he found a combination of gelatine and silver bromide that had the photo-graphic qualities that he sought. Initally, he experimented to sup-port his hobby of photography, but he soon realized that there was commercial potential in what he was doing.

By June 1879, Eastman was manufacturing quality photo-graphic plates and had designed and built equipment for coating them. He obtained his first patent in England, the center of the pho-tographic industry, on July 22, 1879. His patent attorney, George Selden, submitted an application to the U.S. Patent Office for him on September 9, 1879, for "an Improved Process of Preparing Gelatine Dry Plates for Use in Photography and in Apparatus therefor." In April, 1880, he leased the third floor of a building on State Street in Rochester and began to produce dry plates in quan-tity.

A near-fatal catastrophy struck the new business in 1881—photographers complained that Eastman dry plates were no longer sensitive and did not capture an image. Customers discovered something that wasn't realized until then: passage of time lessened the sensitiveness of the emulsion on the plate. The distributor in

New York City had placed the newly received plates on top of the older plates, and had sold the new plates before using up all of the old. By the time the older plates were sold, they had lost their photographic sensitivity. At significant expense for a small company, Eastman recalled all plates and replaced them.

Then, Eastman encountered a second staggering blow—he could no longer make a satisfactory emulsion. During many weeks of sleepless nights with his factory shut down, Eastman conducted 469 unsuccessful experiments to produce a usable emulsion. On March 11, 1882, Eastman and Colonel Henry Alva Strong, the first president of Eastman's company, sailed for England. In England, they discovered that the problem was due to a defective supply of gelatin received from the supplier; it was not a problem with the emulsion formula or Eastman's equipment. They returned on April 16, conducted sixteen more unsuccessful experiments, and were successful on the seventeenth try. Eastman learned two lessons from this experience—to test samples of material received and to control the supply, whenever practical.

 **No Room at the Inn**

obert Green Ingersoll, the foremost orator of his day, was born on August 11, 1833, in Dresden on Seneca Lake. Later in life, while living in Illinois, Ingersoll was a successful lawyer, politician, and philanthropist, but he was principally known as the "Great Infidel." He didn't believe in organized religion or that there could be proof that God exists, but he didn't deny the existence of God. Ingersoll claimed that he didn't understand the concept of hell.

However, those who knew him saw his positive side. A Rochester *Democrat* columnist wrote that "Robert G. Ingersoll is not orthodox in theory, but we should like to see a better Christian in practice ... It is really so nice an article of infidelity that a good deal of it might be passed around with entire safety."

One winter evening after the Civil War, Frederick Douglass, the publisher and antislavery leader, traveled to Peoria. He told a friend that he dreaded going to Peoria because no hotel there would give him a room. On a previous trip, he walked the streets all night to keep from freezing. Douglass' friend told him to contact Robert Ingersoll, who would take him in anytime, day or night. His reception at the Ingersoll home "would have been cordial to the most bruised heart of any proscribed and stormbeaten stranger." Douglass couldn't understand the negative feelings of many people toward the "Great Infidel."

A friend observed, "Whoever crossed the threshhold of the home of Robert G. Ingersoll entered paradise." Mrs. James G. Blaine, after a stay with the Ingersolls, said, "Perhaps I never felt so welcome anywhere in my life." Parker Pillsbury, the abolitionist, observed, "It's a perfect atmosphere of love from the head of the family on down. Even the horse enters into it and seems to appreciate it."

Chapter 10

Ordinary Stories / Observations

Cortland's Presidential Candidate

Alton B. Parker, the Democratic Party's candidate for President of the United States in 1904, was born in Cortland on May 14, 1852. He graduated from Albany Law School in 1873, and practiced law in Kingston. He was a delgate to the Democratic National Convention in 1884. Parker was appointed chairman of the State Democratic Committee and successfully managed the campaign of Elmira's David Hill for governor. He was appointed to a vacant seat on the state supreme court, selected for the court of appeals in 1889, and appointed to the appellate division of the supreme court in 1896. In 1897, he was elected Chief Justice of the court of appeals by a surprising plurality of over 60,000 votes.

Beginning in 1895, he turned down several opportunities to be his party's candidate for governor. In court, he tended to be a liberal judge. For example, he upheld the right of labor unions to obtain a closed shop by threatening to strike, and he upheld the constitutionality of an act limiting the hours of work in bakeries. After the second defeat of Presidential candidate William Jennings Bryan in 1900, the Democrats looked for a new candidate from the eastern wing of the party in 1904. Parker was popular in New York, and he had not been involved in factional differences within the party.

In order not to compromise his position as a judge or to appear to be seeking the nomination for President, he declined to make any statements on public issues before the national convention. He was told that his reticence might cost him the nomination. However, Parker was nominated on the first ballot. During the campaign, his liberal record was downplayed, and he was presented as reliable and conservative.

The Republican candidate for President was Theodore Roosevelt. He had been elected Vice President in 1900 and became President when President McKinley was assassinated. Teddy Roosevelt was young, dynamic, and was known as the hero of the Rough Riders at San Juan Hill in Cuba during the Spanish-American War. Parker received 140 electoral votes to President Roosevelt's 336. Parker was no match for Teddy, whom historians consider one of the five near-great Presidents of the United States.

The Destruction of One-Third of the Ford Tractors in the Ukraine

Dr. Konstantin Frank, who showed that Vitis Vinifera (European) grapes could be grown in the Finger Lakes Region, immigrated to the United States from the Ukraine in 1951. He studied winemaking and grapegrowing at the Polytechnic Institute in Odessa and later worked at the Institute of Enology and Viticulture of the Ukraine.

While working at the Institute, he was responsible for the first three Ford tractors received in the Ukraine from the United States. He decided to determine how heavy a load the tractors could pull. Instead of lining up the tractors side by side, allowing each tractor to pull one-third of the load, he hooked them up in tandem. The back of tractor one was connected to the front of tractor two and tractor three was hitched between the rear of tractor two and the load.

When all three tractors strained to pull the heavy load, they were structurally not up to it. Tractor three, attached to the load, was literally pulled apart and destroyed. Some of the metal parts were stretched, some were broken, and the tractor was beyond repair.

This occurred in the 1930s during the reign of Josef Stalin, and Dr. Frank was concerned about the repercussions of destroying

one-third of the Ukraine's Ford tractors. He wasn't sure how far up the chain of command the information was passed, but nothing happened; no one ever reprimanded him for the incident. Perhaps Stalin was too busy purging the officer corps of the Red Army to pay attention to Soviet agricultural activities.

How Chester A. Arthur Was Nominated Vice President of the U.S.

n June 8, 1880, James A. Garfield received the Republican nomination for President of the United States on the thirty-sixth ballot. He was a dark horse candidate who had emerged because of a deadlock between James G. Blaine and Ulysses S. Grant. The contest at the convention in Chicago was one of the most bitter up until that time.

Garfield's and his campaign manager's first choice for the nomination for Vice President was Levi P. Morton of New York City. Morton was a wealthy banker and importer and, since 1878, a member of Congress. He was commonly considered a "sound money" man. Morton had the backing of both eastern businessmen and the "Half-Breeds," who had supported James G. Blaine for the Presidential nomination.

Senator Roscoe Conkling, an influential New York power broker, was a member of the "Stalwarts" who supported Ulysses S. Grant's nomination for President. Since the Stalwart candidate had lost the nomination for President, Garfield's political advisors decided to chose a Stalwart as the nominee for Vice President. The Garfield supporters offered the nomination for Vice President to Morton, who looked for Conkling to obtain his approval. Morton was unable to find Conkling, and Garfield's advisors became impatient because the delegates were eager for a decision.

After a brief wait for Morton's response, Garfield's advisors offered the nomination for Vice President to Chester A. Arthur, who was also backed by the Stalwarts. Arthur accepted the nomination immediately, without waiting for Conkling's approval. Conkling was angry that he had not been consulted on the decision.

Arthur looked for Conkling and finally found him in the press room of the convention hall. Arthur informed Conkling that he had been offered the nomination for Vice President by Garfield's supporters. The Senator responded in a loud voice, "Well, sir, you should drop it as you would a red-hot shoe from the forge." Arthur replied, "I sought you to consult, not—." Conkling interrupted him, "What is there to consult about? This trickster of Mentor [Garfield] will be defeated before the country."

Arthur told the Senator that there was more to be considered. Conkling was astounded that Arthur was even thinking about accepting the nomination. Arthur replied in a serious tone, "The office of Vice President is a greater honor than I ever dreamed of obtaining. A barren nomination would be a great honor. In a calmer moment you will look at this differently."

The Senator told him, "If you wish for my favor and my respect you will contemptuously decline it." Arthur looked at the power broker directly and said, "Senator Conkling, I shall accept the nomination and I shall carry with me the majority of the delegation." In a rage, Conkling turned his back on Arthur and walked away.

Garfield and Arthur won the 1880 election and were inaugurated as President and Vice President of the United States. On July

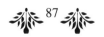

2, 1881, Charles Giteau, a disappointed office seeker, shot President Garfield and cried out, "I am a Stalwart of the Stalwarts ... Arthur is President now." On September 19, 1881, Garfield died, and Arthur was sworn in as the twenty-first President of the United States.

Morton, the cautious banker, had hesitated when offered the Republican nomination for Vice President. Arthur, a man of decision, had responded immediately when offered the nomination and, within a year, was elevated to the highest office in the land.

 ## Millard Fillmore's Carriage

n July 9, 1850, President Zachary Taylor died and Vice President Millard Fillmore was sworn in as President of the United States on the following day. President Taylor had stood in the hot sun during the dedication ceremony beginning the construction of the Washington Monument. He returned to the White House, ate a large quantity of sour cherries, and drank several glasses of cold milk. This may or may not have contributed to his contracting a fever and dying that evening.

The new President thought that he should have a fancy new carriage. "Old Edward" Moran, a White House attendant, had heard of a fine carriage that was for sale because its owner was moving from Washington. President Fillmore was impressed with the carriage, but he had one reservation about buying it. He said, "This is all very well, Edward, but how would it do for the President of the United States to ride around in a second-hand carriage?" Edward replied, "But, sure, your Excellency is only a second-hand President." President Fillmore (the only President born in the Finger Lakes Region) bought the carriage, and it served him well.

The Man Who Could Have Been President

lihu Root, considered by historians to have been one of the most effective Secretaries of War and Secretaries of State during the first half of the twentieth century, was born in Clinton, New York, but spent over four of his formative years in Seneca Falls. He played a significant role in promoting international peace, and, in 1912, he was awarded the Nobel Peace Prize.

On July 21, 1899, President McKinley asked Root to become his Secretary of War. The President assured Root that he needed his legal talents and ability to resolve problems, not his military knowledge or experience. Root followed a well-intentioned but weak Secretary of War. He was immediately confronted with a myriad of challenges, including restoring the reputation of the War Department, providing an army to put down an insurrection in the Philippine Islands, and providing a colonial policy for the United States after its victory in the Spanish-American War.

Root immediately took charge of the War Department. His logical, probing mind coupled with his industry and administrative ability produced early results. He granted a measure of self-government to Hawaii and began to deal with problems in Puerto Rico, Cuba, and the Philippines.

Root's biggest challenge was re-establishing peace in the Philippines and preparing the islands for self-rule. On February 4, 1899, Emilio Aguinaldo led an insurrection against the U.S. troops in the Philippines. Most of these 21,000 troops were due for discharge and had to be replaced with a new army with an authorized strength of 65,000. By early 1900, Aquinaldo was reduced to guerrilla activity by a successful military action planned by Major General Elwell Otis.

In December, 1899, Root was offered the Republican nomination for Vice President for the election in 1900. He declined the nomination to continue with the job that he had just begun in July. He was faced with critical challenges not only in the Philippines, but also in Cuba and Puerto Rico. He chose not to leave unfinished

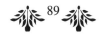

the tasks that he had just undertaken. Theodore Roosevelt accepted the Republican nomination for Vice President in 1900 and was elected to the office for the second term of President McKinley.

On September 6, 1901, President McKinley was shot by Leon Czolgosz, an anarchist, at the Pan-American Exposition in Buffalo. McKinley died on September 14, and Theodore Roosevelt became the twenty-sixth President of the United States. If Root had been less dedicated to his duties, he would have been the Vice President of the United States instead of Theodore Roosevelt. Elihu Root was the man who could have been President.

 ### Red Jacket's Two Suits

wnership of the land was one of the points of disagreement between the Iroquois Confederation and the young government of the United States. Nathaniel Gorham and Oliver Phelps had paid the Native Americans $5,000 in a lump sum and $500 annually for a large part of the Finger Lakes Region. Understandably, the question of ownership persisted with the Iroquois.

President Washington invited the leading Seneca chiefs to Philadelphia, the nation's capital at the time, to discuss their concerns with him, Secretary of War Knox, and Colonel Pickering, the principal negotiator with the Indians. Fifty chiefs made the trip to Philadelphia, including Farmer's Brother and Red Jacket. The discussions went well, and, when they were concluded, the U.S. Government passed a bill to appropriate $1,500 annually to be used to purchase farm animals, clothing, and agricultural implements for the Senecas.

Secretary Knox was directed to provide each chief with a military uniform, a hat, and a sword. Red Jacket was pleased to receive these gifts as were all of the other chiefs. Red Jacket told the quartermaster that he was a man of peace, and that the military uniform and weapon were not suitable for him. He said that, since he wasn't a warrior, he would prefer a plain suit. The quartermaster agreed to that and obtained a civilian suit for Red Jacket. Red Jacket tried it on, and it fit well.

The quartermaster told Red Jacket that he would take back the military uniform. Red Jacket responded that although he was a man of peace, he might at times have to be a warrior. On those occasions, he pointed out that he would need a military uniform. The quartermaster shook his head and walked away. That is how Red Jacket obtained two new suits rather than the one received by the other chiefs.

 ### Red Jacket and the Bear

n several occasions, the bravery of Chief Red Jacket was questioned. This was partly due to the fact that he didn't take up arms until he was twenty-nine years old, and then it was to defend his home territory. When his abilities as a warrior were questioned, he always replied that he was an orator, not a warrior.

One day Red Jacket was traveling from his village on Canandaigua Lake to Seneca Castle, just north of Seneca Lake, with Chief Little Billy and two other braves. Along the way, they encountered a large bear. Little Billy and the two other braves began to run as fast as they could. They knew that they didn't have to outrun the bear; they just had to outrun their slowest companion. Red Jacket, who was skilled with a rifle, stood his ground and shot and killed the bear.

Later, in the presence of other chiefs at a council, Chief Little Billy called Red Jacket a coward and questioned his courage. Red Jacket, who was never at a loss for words, turned to Chief Little Billy and told the council the story about the bear. He then added, "Well, if I'm a coward I never run unless it's for something bigger than a bear." Little Billy was humiliated. It was the last time that he called Red Jacket a coward or questioned his bravery.

Two Blowouts between Elmira and Ithaca

Frank Gannett, the founder of the Gannett newspaper empire, began his chain of newspapers with the Elmira *Star-Gazette*. His first opportunity to expand was an offer to buy the Ithaca *Journal*, for which Gannett had been a reporter earning three dollars a week while a student at Cornell University. Two estates had inherited the *Journal* when its owner passed away, and neither estate had any interest in running a newspaper. Gannett obtained a loan from the Cobb family, who also became part owners, to buy the Ithaca newspaper.

Gannett didn't move to Ithaca to manage the *Journal*; he stayed in Elmira. However, on most weekends, he drove his Willys-Overland motorcar over the hilly road, now known as Route 13, between the two cities. The trip can be made in just over a half-hour today, but in 1912, it was an adventure. Gannett sometimes made the trip alone, but usually Arthur Cochrane, the composing room foreman of the *Star-Gazette*, accompanied him. One of their trips between Elmira and Ithaca took nine hours.

Frequently, a tire would blow out on the trip. Gannett would repair the inner tube with a patch and cement, and then he and Cochrane would struggle to mount the tire and inner tube back on the rim. Gannett worked the pump, and it was Cochrane's responsibility to yell "stop" when the inner tube was sufficiently filled with air.

When Cochrane was nervous, he stuttered. On one trip he was particularly nervous. By the time he could say "ssss-sss-sss-stop" the inner tube blew out, and Gannett had to apply another patch. Again, they wrestled the inner tube and tire on the rim and Gannett resumed pumping. A second time, Cochrane said "ssss-sss-sss-stop" and another blowout occurred. They patched the tube one more time.

Gannett was exasperated, but with infinite patience he turned to his companion and said, "This time, Art, suppose you tell me 'halt' instead of 'stop.'"

 ## Winston Churchill's New York State Ancestors

ost people are aware that Winston Churchill's parents were Lord Randolph Churchill of England and Jennie Jerome of New York. However, many people aren't aware that his mother's grandfather and father were from the Finger Lakes Region. Churchill's maternal great-grandfather, Ambrose Hall, was a State Assemblyman from Wayne County and a highway commissioner in Palmyra in the 1820s.

Churchill's father-in-law, Leonard Jerome, was born south of Syracuse in Pompey, lived on Canal Street in Palmyra, and later resided on a farm in Marion. Ambrose and Clarissa Hall had two daughters, Katherine and Clarissa, who married two brothers, Lawrence and Leonard Jerome from Marion. Leonard Jerome studied at Princeton University for two years, transferred to Union College, and graduated in 1839.

Upon his graduation, he read law in his uncle Hiram Jerome's law office in Palmyra. Hiram moved to Rochester in 1842, and, in 1844, employed Lawrence and Leonard in his law office there. Lawrence Jerome and Katherine Hall were married in August of 1844; Leonard Jerome and Clarissa Hall were married in Palmyra in April of 1849. Both Lawrence and Leonard left the law in 1845 when they bought part interest in the Rochester *Daily American*, a Whig newspaper. They sold their interest in the newspaper in 1850.

Leonard Jerome moved to Brooklyn in 1850, and worked in the fast-growing telegraph industry. Since his daughter, Jennie Jerome, who married Winston Churchill's father, was born in Brooklyn, that area is usually associated with the Jerome family; the memory of Churchill's Wayne County heritage has faded.

Chapter 11

Reminiscences / Rivalries

The Creator of Happy Endings

ary Jane Holmes was born in Brookfield, Massachusetts, on April 5, 1828. She was a precocious child who began attending school at the age of three. Mary Jane, who had a sensitive nature, heard strange voices and had unusual visions. Neighbors wondered what the future held for the dreamy young girl. In her autobiographical novel, *Rice Corners*, she wrote, "I was a strange girl. When forgetful of others, I talked aloud to my band of little folks, unseen 'tis true, but still real to me...."

She taught in the district school in Brookfield when she was only thirteen. Two years later, she left home to live with her uncle, Lyman Hawes, near Honeoye. She taught at the Allen's Hill school for four years. In 1849, she married Daniel Holmes, a young Honeoye lawyer. They moved to Versailles, Kentucky, where Daniel practiced law. After a few years, they returned to Honeoye, and Mary Jane resumed teaching at the Allen's Hill school. After two years in Honeoye, they moved to Canandaigua, where Daniel taught at the Canandaigua Academy and practiced law part-time. In 1853, they moved to Brockport, which was to be their home for the rest of their lives.

Mary Jane and Daniel lived in a cottage on College Street, where Mary Jane wrote thirty-eight romantic novels over a fifty-one year period. Her first novel, *Tempest and Sunshine*, a tale of southern society based on her Kentucky experiences, was published in 1854 and was an immediate success. She wrote from one to three books a year most years from 1854 through 1905 and earned an average of $6,000 for her novels, a substantial amount of money in the last half of the nineteenth century. She also wrote stories for magazines, such as the New York *Weekly*, and many of her novels were serialized in New York periodicals.

Although she lived in Brockport from 1853 until her death in 1907, the scenes of most of her novels were New England, the South, and Europe. She occasionally wrote about Saratoga Springs and about Madison Square in New York City, but she rarely wrote about Genesee Country. One exception was *Cousin Maude*, in which the heroine travels from New England to Canandaigua. She is met at the train station and transported by farm wagon to Laurel Hill, "from whose rocky hillsides she can see the sparkling waters of Honeoye."

Holme's novels would not be popular with today's readers. Her writing is not subtle, her characters are described rather briefly, and, of course, there is no sex and violence. Her heroes were wonderful people of strong character, and her villains were described in a way that caused the nineteenth-century reader to want to boo and hiss. She always wove a love interest into her novels. When asked why, she responded, "I write what people want." The readers of Holme's novels always expected a happy ending; she never disappointed them.

Holmes traveled widely around the United States as well as in Africa, Asia, Canada, and Europe. She and Daniel lived in Sweden and Norway for four years and spent their summers in France and the Holy Land. She gleaned material during her travels for her books that were set in Europe.

Holmes was active in community affairs in Brockport. She tithed her income to charity and religious causes. She established a free reading room in Brockport, assisted with the financing of St. Luke's parish house, and provided support for many needy families. The author was head of the Union Benevolent Society and president of her church guild. She was a regent of the Daughters of the American Revolution and was an active member of the Women's Christian Temperance Union.

Mary Jane Holmes died on October 6, 1907, in her cottage in Brockport. Her life, like those in her stories, ended well. Nearly 1,000 people walked by her bier in St. Luke's Episcopal Church,

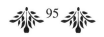

where she had worshipped for over fifty years. Daniel died in 1919. Up until his death, he was the sole surviving member of the original board of the Brockport Normal School (now State University of New York—College at Brockport). When his estate was settled, Mary Jane's jewelry was sold and the proceeds given to three Rochester-area charities: the Episcopal Church Home, the Orphan Asylum, and the Industry School.

The Dreams of Chief Hendrick and Sir William Johnson

ntil he died in 1774, Sir William Johnson, who was called Warraghiyagey—The-Man-Who-Undertakes-Great-Things—by the Iroquois, was the Superintendent of Indian Affairs for the crown of England. The Iroquois liked him, and he exerted a strong, moderating influence on English / Native American relations. He was knighted by the King of England and accumulated significant wealth when he was given the opportunity to purchase Indian lands.

Shortly after he was appointed Superintendent of Indian Affairs, he ordered several expensive, colorfully embroidered suits of clothing. He wanted to project an authoritative image to the Native Americans. Chief Hendrick, a Mohawk sachem, was at Sir William's home on the Mohawk River when the suits arrived from England. The chief admired the suits and could not get them out of his mind.

Chief Hendrick returned the following day and told Sir William that he had dreamed that Sir William had given him one of richly embroidered suits. Sir William felt obligated to give one of his prized possessions to Chief Hendrick. The chief left Sir William's home immediately to show his friends his new clothing. Sir William told his friends that he lost one of his new suits because he couldn't refuse the chief.

The next time that Sir William saw Chief Hendrick, he told him, "Hendrick, I have dreamed a dream." Unsuspectingly, Chief Hendrick asked, "And what did you dream?" Sir William told the chief that he had dreamed that he had given him a parcel of land, which was 500 acres of the most valuable land in the Mohawk Valley. Chief Hendrick shook his head and responded, "It is yours; Sir William, I will never dream with you again." If this story is representative, it is easy to see how Sir William Johnson became wealthy.

The Story of the Gift of Trees

hen the Iroquois first arrived on the earth, they were welcomed by the trees. The trees offered up many gifts that supplied the Iroquois with things that helped them to live. They used the bark of the Elm tree for containers in which to store corn that the Great Spirit had given to them to sustain them. They also made bowls from Elm bark in which to mix their corn pudding.

The Maple tree gave them its sweet sap with which to make maple syrup to drink and to flavor their food. They also made bowls and buckets from wood of the trunk of the Maple to use in collecting the sap. The Oak tree was used to make the rugged corn pounder that the Native Americans used to crush the kernels into corn meal. They formed hollow logs out of Oak and other hardwoods to use in boiling Maple sap into Maple sugar and for other cooking uses.

The Iroquois formed the bows that they used for hunting from the Ash tree, which also gave the them the sturdy, flexible strips that could be woven into baskets. The various nut trees provided them with food to put into the baskets. The Hickory tree offered straight boughs from which arrows could be made. They made their canoes from the strong, pliable bark of the White Birch. They used Pine pitch to bind the pieces of Birch together and help make the canoes watertight. The Pine tree also provided them soft, fragrant boughs on which to sleep. Their early lodges were constructed of Pine bark.

The Native Americans rubbed two sticks from the Fir tree together to start fires to provide heat and light for longhouses and

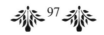

to cook food. They believed that the trees could understand them and should be treated gently. They also believed that they learned the gift of giving from the trees.

The Story of Lebbeus Hammond

ne spring day in Pennsylvania late in the eighteenth century, Thomas Bennett and his son, Andrew, were captured by Indians while plowing their fields. As their party walked north towards New York State, they joined another party of Native Americans who were traveling with a fellow captive, Lebbeus Hammond. After traveling for three days, the prisoners were told that they would be killed on the following day.

Lebbeus and Thomas planned to escape from their captors during that night. They realized that attempting to escape would be risky, but they didn't have much to lose. If they didn't escape, the next day would be their last.

That night, the two men and the boy were "papoosed." They were told to lie on the ground, and saplings were bent over and tied in place above them. Indians slept at the openings at the ends of the bent saplings to prevent their escape. During the middle of the night, Thomas told his captors that he was sick. He asked to be allowed to get up, but the Indians ignored him. Finally, he made such a fuss that he woke the entire camp.

The Indians were so eager to get back to sleep that they didn't retie the saplings over their captives; they left an old brave to guard them. The guard roasted bits of venison over the camp fire, and then fell asleep after he had filled his stomach. Sneaking up behind the sleeping guard, Thomas struck him a fatal blow with a heavy spear, but not before the Indian had alarmed the camp.

Lebbeus used an ax to kill the first Indian to come to the guard's aid. Using the Indians' own weapons, the two men and the boy were soon in control of the camp. Only two Native Americans escaped, and one of them received a heavy tomahawk blow to the head from Lebbeus. Years later, Lebbeus saw this Indian at the signing of the Treaty of Painted Post. He had a deep scar and was unable hold up his head. Lebbeus' children and grandchildren lived in Chemung county, and those living in the Elmira area have passed the story down from one generation to the next.

The Story of the Peace Queen

he Iroquois chose a Seneca maiden known for her good judgment to act as a judge in settling disputes for all of the nations in the confederation. They provided her with a lodge deep in the forest. Seneca squaws considered her to be a sacred being. Her word was the law and could not be contested.

One afternoon while hunting in the woods, an Oneida brave killed a buck with one arrow through the heart. As he was removing the skin from the deer and was about to cut it into quarters, an Onondaga brave stepped out from the trees and said that the kill belonged to him. He claimed that he had fatally wounded the buck before the Oneida brave shot his arrow to finish him off. Their argument became heated, and they fought for several hours with neither gaining the advantage over the other.

Finally, the two exhausted braves decided to present their disagreement to Genetaska, the Peace Queen, for resolution. She scolded them for fighting within her domain, directed them to divide the deer equally, and told them to return to their villages. However, the Onondaga brave was smitten with beauty of the Peace Queen and didn't want to return to his home. He proposed to her and asked her to share his lodge. She told him that she could not marry because of her sacred duty to the Iroquois Confederation. The saddened Onondaga brave prepared to return to his village.

The Oneida brave also had fallen in love with the Peace Queen. She refused his offer of marriage also, but she responded so softly and affectionately that he couldn't get her out of his mind.

She asked the two braves to leave in peace. They were reconciled and became friends with the common bond of unrequited love for the same woman.

However, Genetaska thought about the Oneida brave all the time—upon waking, during the day, and while going to sleep in the evening. Many moons passed, and the Peace Queen fulfilled her obligation to the Iroquois to settle disputes. However, her heart was saddened with longing for the brave, gentle Oneida warrior.

One day she pined for him as she warmed herself by the fire, and he appeared before her. He looked pale and haggard and explained that he could not live without her. He had lost interest in the hunt, and he no longer enjoyed playing lacrosse and other games with his friends. He admitted that the light had gone out of his life, and he asked again for her hand in marriage. This time, she agreed to become his wife. She regretted walking away from her sacred obligations, but she knew that she would wither away if she didn't marry the one that she loved. She and her brave traveled eastward toward their new home.

The chiefs who had elected her Peace Queen to settle disputes were angry with her for abandoning her duties and responsibilities. They tore down her lodge in the woods and abolished the position of Peace Queen. No one was elected to take her place. As might be expected, arguments, fights, and wars resumed within the Iroquois Confederation.

Whose Airplane Was Really the First to Fly

amuel Langley's *Great Aerodrome*

Samuel Langley, the Secretary (Director) of the Smithsonian Institution, attempted heavier-than-air flight just before the Wright Brothers' successful flight of the *Flyer* at Kitty Hawk, North Carolina, on December 17, 1903. Because Langley was then in his sixties and had a heavy build, he contracted Charles Manley, the Cornell-educated engineer who had designed the *Great Aerodrome's* engine, to be the pilot.

On October 8th, 1903, the biplane with Manley aboard was catapulted from a houseboat on the Potomac. Busy with his responsibilities back at the Smithsonian, Langley was not present for the test flight. Manley headed into a five-mile-per-hour wind; however, a part of the aircraft caught on the launching device and the plane was projected downward. It came to rest in sixteen feet of water about 150 feet from the houseboat. Manley was unharmed.

Photographs were used to evaluate the causes of the failure. The 42-foot wings that provided a wing area of 1,040 square feet were insufficiently braced and showed the strain of attempting to lift the 850-pound load of airplane, engine, and pilot. As had been suspected, a failure of the launching mechanism that caused it to snag the aircraft as it prepared to take off was the main problem. Other causes were structural deficiencies and shortcomings with the control mechanisms. Although funds almost exhausted and winter was approaching, Langley decided to rebuild the aircraft and try one more flight.

On December 8, 1903, Langley was present at the second launch of the *Great Aerodrome* from the houseboat on the Potomac. The craft hung up again on the launch rail and Manley said that: " ... just before the machine left the launching car he felt an extreme swaying motion immediately followed by a tremendous jerk which caused the machine to quiver all over ..." The support wires connecting the tail and rear wings snapped, the aircraft turned upward, and fell backward into the water. A third flight was not attempted; Langley did not have the funds to continue with his experiments.

The Wright Brothers' *Flyer*

On December 17th, 1903, at Kitty Hawk, North Carolina, the temperature was freezing and the wind was blowing at twenty-seven miles per hour. It was Orville's turn to pilot the airplane; the brothers shook hands as though they weren't going to see each other again. At 10:35 a.m., the *Flyer* lifted about forty feet above the ground and flew 120 feet in twelve seconds.

The Wrights considered this flight to be the true first flight. Orville commented, "This flight lasted only twelve seconds, but it was nevertheless the first in the history of the world in which a

machine carrying a man had raised itself by its own power into the air in full flight, had sailed forward without a reduction in speed, and had finally landed at a point as high as that from which it started."

Wilbur flew the second flight of the day over a distance of 175 feet, followed by Orville in a flight of over 200 feet that lasted fifteen seconds. Wilbur flew the *Flyer* on the last flight of the day— a flight of 852 feet with a duration of 59 seconds. While they were discussing the flights, a gust of wind overturned the *Flyer*, breaking spars, struts, most of the wing ribs, and the engine crankcase. No more flights were conducted in 1903. However, the Wright brothers had accomplished their goal. They had ushered in powered flight.

The "Reconstruction" of the *Great Aerodrome* by Glenn Curtiss

Glenn Curtiss of Hammondsport, who had traded aircraft design information with the Wright Brothers, was accused by them of infringing on their wing-warping control system patents. The U.S. Court of Appeals, Second Circuit, upheld the Wright Brothers' claim.

In April 1914, Dr. C. Walcott, Langley's successor as Secretary of the Smithsonian Institution, gave Curtiss permission to reconstruct the *Great Aerodrome* to determine whether it was capable of flight. Curtiss transported Langley's aircraft to Hammondsport to rebuild it. Along with substantial other changes, Curtiss added floats to the *Great Aerodrome* and flew the aircraft off Keuka Lake at Hammondsport on May 28, 1914, and again on June 2, 1914. The longest flight off the water with the fifty-two-horsepower Langley engine lasted only five seconds.

When Curtiss returned the aircraft, Walcott reinstalled it in the Smithsonian Institution and published the statement that the *Great Aerodrome* was "the first aeroplane capable of sustained free flight with a man." This statement contradicted the Wright Brothers' claim for their *Flyer*. Walcott's statement was misleading because he didn't mention that Curtiss had made many changes to Langley's aircraft during the restoration. The fact that Curtiss had lost a patent suit to the Wright Brothers clouded the issue further.

Because of this controversy, Orville Wright—Wilbur had died in 1912—refused to allow the *Flyer* to be displayed in the Smithsonian Institution. Secretary Walcott died in 1927, and his successor, Dr. C. G. Abbott, also refused to give the proper recognition to the Wright Brothers for their historic acomplishment. In 1928, Orville Wright sent the *Flyer* to the Science Museum in London, where it was exhibited, except for the World War II years, until 1948.

Curtiss had made many changes to Langley's *Great Aerodrome*, including:
- Reducing the wing width from 11' 6" to 10' 11 3/4," which reduced the wing area from 1,040 to 988 square feet
- Increasing the aspect ratio from 1.96 to 2.05
- Changing the camber from 1 / 12 to 1 / 18
- Varnishing the cotton fabric covering, which was unvarnished on the 1903 flights
- Replacing most of the ribs of the hollow box construction
- Using a different system of wing trussing
- Replacing the two-surface split vane rudder with a single plane vertical rudder
- Adding a rudder that served as a vertical aileron and a Penaud tail rudder for lateral stability in addition to the dihedral angle used by Langley
- Supplementing the Penaud system with an elevator system of control for longitudinal stability
- Modifying the five-cylinder Langley motor
- Replacing the dry cell batteries used in the ignition system with a magneto
- Exchanging the Balzer carburetor with a float-feed automobile carburetor
- Replacing the radiator constructed of tubes with radiating fins with a honeycomb-type automobile radiator
- Modifying the propellers "after a fashion of early Wright blades"
- Replacing the keel under the mainframe that was used with a catapult with two wooden hydroplane floats
- Changing the aircraft's center of gravity

- Increasing the total weight of the aircraft with a pilot from 850 to 1170 pounds

When Orville Wright threatened to leave the *Flyer* in London permanently and to modify his will to ensure that it stayed there, the Smithsonian Institution knew that it had been beaten. On October 24, 1942, Abbott published a paper, *The 1914 Tests of the Langley Aerodrome*, which included the following apology:

> Since I became Secretary in 1928, I have made many efforts to compose the Smithsonian-Wright controversy, which I inherited. I will now, speaking for the Smithsonian Institution, make the following statement in an attempt to correct as far as now possible acts and assertions of former Smithsonian officials that may have been misleading or are held to be detrimental to the Wrights.
>
> 1. I sincerely regret that the Institution employed to make the tests of 1914 an agent who had been an unsuccessful defendant in patent litigation brought against him by the Wrights.
>
> 2. I sincerely regret that statements were repeatedly made by officers of the Institution that the Langley machine was flown in 1914 "with certain changes of the machine necessary to use pontoons," without mentioning the other changes included in Dr. Wright's list.
>
> 3. I point out that Assistant Secretary Rathburn was misinformed when he stated that the Langley machine "without modifications" made "successful flights."
>
> 4. I sincerely regret the public statement by officers of the Institution that "The Tests" [of 1914] showed "that the late Secretary Langley had succeeded in building the first aeroplane capable of sustained free flight with a man."
>
> 5. Leaving to experts to formulate the conclusions arising from the 1914 tests as a whole, in view of all the facts, I repeat in substance, but with amendments, what I have already pub-

lished in *Smithsonian Scientific Series*, Vol. 12, 1932, page 227:

"The flights of the Langley aerodrome at Hammondsport in 1914, having been made long after flying had become a common art, and with changes of the machine indicated by Dr. Wright's comparison as given above, did not warrant the statements published by the Smithsonian Institution that these tests proved that the large Langley machine of 1903 was capable of sustained flight carrying a man."

6. If the publication of this paper should clear the way for Dr. Wright to bring back to America the Kitty Hawk machine to which all the world awards first place, it will be a source of profound and enduring gratification to his countrymen everywhere. Should he decide to deposit the plane in the United States National Museum, it would be given the highest place of honor, which is its due.

On December 17, 1948, the Smithsonian Institution held a formal ceremory to welcome the *Flyer* back to Washington, D.C. Unfortunately, Orville Wright was not there; he had died on the previous January 30. After being out of the country for twenty years, the historic Wright aircraft was finally back home where it belonged.

Chapter 12

Inventions / Ideas

The Development of the Sound-on-Film System

Theodore Willard Case, pioneer in motion picture sound synchronization, lived at 203 Genesee Street, Auburn. His mansion now houses the Cayuga Museum of History and Art. Theodore Case and William Fox formed the Fox-Case Movietone Corporation, which was part of the studio that became Twentieth Century Fox.

The Case Research Laboratory was located in Theodore Case's mansion, and the sound studio was in the carriage house. In the laboratory, Theodore Case and E.I. Sponable invented the first commercially successful sound-on-film system. This system was used by de Forest Phonofilms Company from 1922 to 1925, and by Fox Films from 1926 to 1937. It preceded the Warner Brothers Vitaphone disc system.

In July 1926, William Fox bought the patent rights to the sound-on-film system developed by Case and Sponable. The Fox-Case Corporation was formed to develop and sell the system called "Movietone."

The developers of sound motion picture systems had been confronted with the challenge of recording and reproducing sounds accurately. Two distinct systems were developed to meet this challenge:

- The disc system, which was similar to a extremely sensitive phonograph record, but was twice as large and ran at half the speed.
- The sound-on-film system in which the sound record was photographed on a sound track on the film itself. The amount of light falling on the film

varied with the microphone current, and the contrast between the light and dark microscopic lines of the sound track captured the loudness of the sound. The greater the contrast, the louder the sound. One of the innovations of the Case / Sponable design was a unique light that they had developed in 1922. It was very sensitive to sound vibrations, thus allowing sound represented by lines to be photographed on the film.

The first use of the Movietone sound-on-film was for the New York premiere of the Fox film, *What Price Glory*. Fox then began to use the Movietone system principally on newsreels. On May 20, 1927, Movietone had its first major success with a newsreel that was in movie theaters within twenty-four hours of Lindberg's take-off from Roosevelt Field on his solo transatlantic flight. The Movietone system was more mobile than its disc counterpart, and eventually it became the preferred system.

The Case Research Laboratory collection in Auburn includes the sound projector that set the standards for today's film industry, the blimp box that housed the camera man, de Forest amplifiers, experimental light cells, laboratory equipment, and Western Electric amplifiers. The collection also includes many test films that were made at the laboratory during the development of sound-on-film systems.

The First McCormick Harvester

n 1831, Cyrus McCormick, a blacksmith from West Virginia, invented a reaper for harvesting wheat. It could harvest as much wheat as seven men harvesting by hand. McCormick spent a number of years in Washington, D.C., obtaining a patent for his invention and improving its design. While in Washington, he met Brockport Congressman E. B. Holmes. McCormick had been looking for someone to manufacture his reapers, and Holmes told him about Brockport's Bacchus and Burroughs foundry that had been manufacturing farm implements since 1828.

In 1844, McCormick moved to Brockport and contracted Bacchus and Burroughs to make 100 harvesters to his design. The inventor encountered problems with the first 100 reapers that were built. However, on Frederick Root's farm in the town of Sweden, one of them became the first machine to harvest wheat in the United States. In 1846, McCormick ordered another 100 harvesters to be built at the small canalside shop of Dayton S. Morgan and William H. Seymour. McCormick was much more satisfied with the second 100 machines. One of these machines is on display in Henry Ford's museum at Greenfield Village in Michigan.

Although the Genesee region had been the wheat basket of the country in the late 1700s and early 1800s, the center of wheat production moved to the Midwest in the late 1800s. McCormick moved to Chicago and became a wealthy man manufacturing his harvesters.

Brockport continued to be a center for the manufacture of farm equipment into the 1890s, when the shift of wheat production to the Midwest was accompanied by the relocation of the manufacturing of farm equipment there.

Frederick Root, on whose farm the first grain had been harvested by machinery, invented a grain cleaner and separator. In 1851, William H. Seymour manufactured the automatic raking reaper, which he called "the quadrant platform." Seymour's old partner, Dayton S. Morgan, manufactured his line of Triumph reapers for twenty years until 1894, when his factory was destroyed by fire.

The Bacchus and Burroughs foundry was taken over by the Johnson Harvester factory, which employed just under 500 people and turned out 6,000 machines during its peak year in 1882. That year the Bacchus and Burroughs factory burned down and manufacturing was moved to Batavia, which presumedly had a more effective fire department than Brockport.

The First Northern Spy Apple

historical marker located one mile north of County Road 3 on Boughton Road in East Bloomfield contains the following message: "Original Northern Spy Apple [tree] stood 14 rods south of this spot in a seedling orchard planted by Herman Chapin about 1800." The Northern Spy apple has a tangy flavor and a tender texture and is popular for making apple pie, apple sauce, and baked apples; it is also considered a good eating apple. The apple's name is rumored to have originated when an early grower commented that he had spied a tree at the northern edge of his orchard that had begun to bear fruit with an unfamiliar, but appealing, flavor.

S. A. Beach summarized the history of the Northern Spy apple in 1905 in *The Apples of New York*:

Originated in a seedling orchard at East Bloomfield, N.Y., which is famous for the production of this variety, the Early Joe, and the Melon. This orchard was planted by Herman Chapin with seedling trees grown from seeds brought from Salisbury, Connecticut, about the year 1800. Sprouts from the original tree were taken up and planted by Roswell Humphrey, and by him the first fruit of the Northern Spy was raised, as the original tree died before bearing. In 1847, nine of the trees were still living.

The variety was confined to the vicinity of its origin for many years, and it was not until about 1840 that it began to attract the attention of fruit growers in other localities. Its great value then came to be more widely recognized, and in 1852 the American Pomological Society not only listed it as a promising new variety but also as a variety worthy of general cultivation. Since that time it has become extensively planted not only in New York but also in other northern apple-growing regions.

For much of the late eighteenth and early twentieth centuries, the Northern Spy was the third most frequently grown apple in New York State, after the Rhode Island Greening and the Baldwin. By 1971, it had dropped to eighth place, only 3.3 percent of the New York State crop, after those two varieties and the McIntosh, Cortland, Rome Beauty, and Red and Golden Delicious.

Since the establishment the New York State Agricultural Experiment Station at Geneva in 1881, many new apple varieties have been introduced. For example, in 1898 the Cortland apple was created by crossing the McIntosh and Ben Davis apples.

Many factors contribute to making New York State, particularly western New York, a major growing area for the apple—a member of the rose family. The climate of cold winters, moderate springs, mild summers, and cool falls is favorable for growing apples, as is the rich, deep, and well-drained soil. By 1971, 72,569 acres of apples were grown in New York State, including 44,206 acres in western New York.

The Formation of the American Red Cross

uring the Civil War, Clara Barton served with distinction both as battlefield nurse and in military hospitals. After the war she collected information on soldiers who were missing in action and succeeded in locating over 22,000 of them. In 1868, on the verge of a nervous breakdown, she went to Europe to rest and stayed with friends in Switzerland.

Dr. Louis Appia of the Red Cross visited her. He was familiar with her work during the Civil War and asked why the United States had three times rejected his offer to join the Red Coss. Barton had not heard of the organization that had been founded by Jean-Henri Dunant. After witnessing the bloody Battle of Solferino, Dunant wrote *A Memory of Solferino*, in which he proposed the formation of an international relief organization. The Swiss-based organization chose for its symbol a red cross on a white background—the reverse of the color scheme of the Swiss flag. Barton began to consider forming a relief organization in the United States.

In 1873, Barton returned home. She spent the next four years convalescing from a nervous disorder that caused migraine headaches and periods of blindness. In March, 1876, she moved to Dansville, New York, to improve her health at a sanatorium called Our Home on the Hillside. After a year's rest with wholesome food in a peaceful environment, Barton completely regained her health. She bought a home and lived for ten years in Dansville, where she made many close friends.

While living in Dansville, Barton worked to bring the United States into the International Red Cross. She discovered that the reason for the resistance in the United States to joining the organization was that it was considered a wartime relief organization. Barton pointed out the need for such an organization in addressing peacetime disasters, such as earthquakes and floods. She went to Washington, D.C., to convince President Garfield's cabinet of the importance of a U.S. role in the international relief organization.

On her return to Dansville, the townspeople asked her to help form a local chapter of the Red Cross. On August 22, 1881, the first American chapter of the Red Cross was established in Dansville. The first disaster addressed by the chapter was a Michigan forest fire that took 500 lives and destroyed 1,500 homes. On March 16, 1882, Congress signed the Treaty of Geneva, which made the U.S. a member of the International Red Cross. Barton was appointed as the first president of the American Red Cross and served in that position until May, 1904. She died in Washington, D.C., on April 12, 1912.

The Founding of the New York *Times*

Henry Jarvis Raymond, the oldest of three sons of Jarvis Raymond and Lavina Brockway Raymond, was born on January 24, 1820, on an eighty-acre farm outside of the village of Lima. He learned to read at the age of three, and he began to attend the district school when he was four. Raymond attended the village grade school until the Genesee Wesleyan Seminary opened in Lima in 1832. He was a member of first class at the seminary, which subsequently was moved to Syracuse and became the nucleus for Syracuse University in 1869.

Raymond worked in a store and taught briefly at the district school in Wheatland prior to enrolling at the University of Vermont in September, 1836. At Burlington, he was an accomplished orator and an avid writer. Some of his early verses were printed in Horace Greeley's first newspaper, *The New Yorker*. In 1840, Greeley hired him as the head of the literary department at *The New Yorker*. In the following year, Greeley founded the New York *Tribune* and appointed Raymond as his assistant. Raymond worked long hours and developed an articulate writing style. He met New York's important journalists and politicians and covered national events for the *Tribune*.

Raymond left the *Tribune* after two years, mainly because, as a conservative, he did not agree with Greeley's support of Socialist

causes. In 1843, he became an editor of the *Courier and Enquirer*, a Whig newspaper published for Wall Street. Raymond became widely known within newspaper circles and within the state Whig party, particularly with party leaders William H. Seward and Thurlow Weed.

In May 1848, Raymond had a key role in creating the Associated Press, a cooperative venture formed to share foreign news and presidential campaign news as well as to reduce the intense rivalry among the New York newspapers. Six New York papers were the original members of the Associated Press: the *Courier,* the *Express*, the *Herald*, the *Journal of Commerce*, the *Sun*, and the *Tribune*. Raymond continued to be an important member of the organization as it grew.

During the 1840s, Raymond and George Jones, an Albany banknote broker, discussed founding a newspaper. By 1846, they prepared a rough draft of a plan to start a new paper. In 1850, Raymond was elected to the State Assembly and had more opportunities to talk with Jones in Albany about their plans. Jones thought that they could start the venture with $40,000, but Raymond thought that $100,000 was a more realistic amount. They found a third partner, Edward B. Wesley, another broker from Albany, to provide the amount that they lacked.

Raymond envisioned a newspaper with a wide circulation emphasizing city news: business news, maritime news, public meetings, religious gatherings, and stock market news. He thought that "the law courts should be carefully, accurately and more fully reported that is usual—as they relate to business, and thus enlist the attention and interest of a very large class of people."

Raymond planned to have two Washington correspondents, and he wanted to be represented in Albany when the legislature was in session. Also, he hired correspondents to cover Baltimore, Boston, Charleston, Montreal, New Orleans, and Philadelphia. The paper would have a correspondent in Paris but would rely on the London press for news from England.

Raymond defined his job as editor:

The editor should see and examine everything that goes into the paper—in every department, and should besides

write such editorials upon matters of news that might be needed. This would serve to fill up and give life to the editorial department. The editor should also take care that nothing immoral should get into any part of the paper and would of course see that all employed as writers, reporters or correspondents worked in such a way as to promote the interest and build up the character of the paper.

On September 17, 1851, the first issue of the New York *Daily Times* was printed on the Hoe presses in its new facility.

Raymond's two main competitors were Horace Greeley's *Tribune* and James Gordon Bennett's *Herald*. He sought the middle ground between the reformist eccentricity of Greeley and the sensationalism of Bennett. The *Daily Times* began as a conservative newspaper with leanings toward the Whigs. Raymond's goal was to make the new publication an authoritive source of information on domestic and foreign affairs that included coverage of financial, political, and social events.

In 1854, Raymond ran for Lieutenant Governor on the Whig ticket with Myron H. Clark of Canandaigua. Clark, the temperance candidate for Governor, and Raymond were elected by a narrow margin. Raymond returned to Albany to preside over the State Senate. While serving in Albany, he played a significant role in the reelection of Seward to the U.S. Senate.

In September, 1855, both the state conventions of the Whig party and the new Republican party met in Syracuse. Greeley, one of the early advocates of the new party, proposed the name "Republican" for it. The two conventions began separately but ended jointly. Raymond became a driving force in the new party. He prepared a draft for the New York delegation to deliver at the 1856 Republican National Convention in Pittsburgh. The convention adopted it unamimously.

Raymond continued to be active in the Republican party and, in 1864, was appointed chairman of the party's National Committee. In addition, he was President Lincoln's campaign manager for his 1864 Presidential campaign. Raymond ran for congress that year and was elected, again, by a narrow margin. He was a good speechmaker for his causes, but he did not excel in the political infighting.

Raymond encountered health problems in his late forties. He began to have problems with his eyesight and he developed a facial twitch. He dropped out of politics but continued to drive himself at the *Times*. In the evening of June 18, 1869, two men supporting a third rang the doorbell at 12 W. Ninth Street, placed the third man on the stoop, and left. Raymond's daughter, Mary, came to the door and was alarmed to find her father breathing heavily and lying on the floor. She sent for a doctor and went next door for help. Apparently, Raymond had suffered a stroke. He died early in the morning of the following day.

Henry Jarvis Raymond had a life full of accomplishments, including assisting in founding the Republican Party and the Associated Press, and having served as Lieutenant Governor, Congressman, national chairman of his party, and as presidential campaign manager for Abraham Lincoln. However, his most significant achievement was to found the New York *Times*. Eventually, the newspaper with the motto "All the News That's Fit to Print" became the country's newspaper of record.

The Invention That Wasn't

George Baldwin Selden, an inventor and patent attorney from a family of lawyers and judges, was born near Clarkson Corners, Monroe County, in 1846. Selden's father, Henry R. Selden, and his uncle, Samuel L. Selden, were both judges on the New York State Court of Appeals, and Henry R. Selden was the state's first Republican lieutenant governor.

According to Rochester historian Blake McKelvey, "As a lad, George B. Selden had been influenced by the practical interest of George Hand Smith [the local inventor of a headlamp for locomotives], and by the mechanical devices employed at the Morgan agricultural implements factory in Brockport...." Selden's technical interests led him to study at Yale University's Scientific School. It was almost inevitable that, having an interest in science and com-

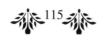

ing from a family of lawyers, Selden would become a patent attorney.

In 1877, Selden completed his design for a gasoline engine for automobiles. Ten years earlier, Dr. N. A. Otto had invented a four-cycle internal combustion engine in Germany that ran on illuminating gas. In 1874, an American inventor, George Brayton, developed a two-cycle engine that was powered by gasoline. Selden's engine design was an adaptation of the Brayton design with six cylinders in an enclosed crankcase, a short piston stroke instead of a long one, and large valves. Selden also designed an automobile in which to mount his engine. Its features included a clutch to allow a choice of speeds, a foot brake, front wheel drive, and a muffler.

On May 8, 1879, Selden applied for a patent for "a safe, simple, and cheap road locomotive possessed of sufficient power to overcome an ordinary inclination." He submitted a brass model of the vehicle, most of which he had built himself, with his application to the U.S. Patent Office. Unfortunately, Selden didn't have the capital to build and promote automobiles using his design. He continued to amend his patent papers, and his final application for patent no. 549,160 for "the application of a compression gas engine to road or horseless carriage use" was not submitted until November 5, 1895.

While Selden was amending his patent, other inventors were catching up with him and passing him. In 1885, Gottlieb Daimler adapted the Otto engine in Germany to run on gasoline. In that same year, Daimler's countryman, Carl Benz, built the first automobile to run on gasoline. Benz convinced a French company to build his three-wheeled automobiles powered by the Daimler engine, and by 1890 hundreds of the vehicles were being produced.

In 1899, Selden still lacked the capital to build his own cars, so he contracted with the Columbia Company of Hartford, Connecticut, to manufacture them. Selden transferred his patent to Columbia in return for royalties on the cars produced. Columbia also attempted to collect royalties on all gasoline-powered cars made in the United States. Many manufacturers refused to honor Selden's patent, and Columbia initiated infringement suits against them. Columbia won the early infringement suits, including the first suit against the Winton Motor Carriage Company.

In 1903, ten of the leading car manufacturers formed the Association of Licensed Automobile Manufacturers to pool their patents and to initiate suits against competitors who infringed on their patents and refused to pay royalties. The association obtained control of Selden's patent and paid him twenty percent of the retail price of all of the automobiles that they sold. By 1910, the association had expanded to eighty-seven members that produced over ninety percent of the automobiles in the United States.

In 1905, Selden mounted an engine made to his design on a chassis built according to the specifications in his patent. He drove the automobile in New York City and in Rochester to demonstrate the practicality of his design. In the following year, Selden obtained $500,000 from Rochester investors to found the Selden Motor Company, and in 1908 drove one of his cars to New York City to seek publicity.

Henry Ford and several other automobile manufacturers had refused to join the Association of Licensed Automobile Manufacturers and paid no royalties to them. A court battle ensued and on September 15, 1909, the United States Circuit Court upheld the association's patent claims that applied to all gasoline-powered automobiles.

Henry Ford and his associates appealed, and, on January 9, 1911, the U.S. Circuit Court of Appeals limited the application of the association's engine patent to two-cycle engines similar to Selden's. However, by this time, all manufacturers were using the four-cycle Otto engine design. In effect, the appeals court had overturned the earlier decision, and Henry Ford had won a resounding victory.

By 1911, Selden had earned $360,000 in royalties, and he retired from the Selden Motor Vehicle Company. Other members of his family continued to operate the company, which concentrated on the manufacture of trucks. The Selden Company was one of two manufacturers commissioned by the U.S. Government to make Liberty trucks for use by the American Expeditionary Force in World War I.

George Selden was financially successful with his patent for a "road locomotive." If the original court ruling that applied to cars with any gasoline-powered engine had been sustained, he would

have become another John D. Rockefeller as the automotive industry experienced explosive growth. However, his invention became, in the words of Columbia University historian John Garraty, "the invention that wasn't."

 **The Misunderstood Bribe**

ethro Wood of Scipio, the inventor of the cast-iron plow, was granted two patents for plows. His first patent was awarded in 1814, but he realized the shortcomings of this plow and destroyed the patterns. The patent granted to him on September 1, 1819, the design for which he sought royalties, was a significant improvement. The improvements in this design were the use of cast iron, the use of three replaceable parts (eliminating the need for sharpening the share), and the means of adjusting the connection of the mould-board and the beam to plow a deeper or shallower furrow. Wood considered the main improvement of his plow to be the use of cast iron. Earlier plows were constructed of wood with a sheet of iron fastened to the mould-board for additional strength.

Wood's patent expired in 1833, and he was granted a extension for fourteen years. He realized very few royalties on his patent, even though plows made to his design were in use all over the country. Wood died in 1834, and his son, Benjamin, took up the struggle to obtain royalties. John Quincy Adams, Henry Clay, and Daniel Webster all attempted to aid Benjamin Wood, but their main accomplishment was to obtain improvements to the patent laws.

The Circuit Court at Albany ruled that the plow in widespread use was, in fact, a unique design invented by Jethro Wood, and that all manufacturers must pay the heirs of Jethro Wood for the use of the design. However, this ruling was made in 1845, and the patent had only one more year to run. Benjamin left immediately for Washington to request a second extension on the patent. The exertion was too much for him, and he died of a heart attack.

Two of Jethro's four daughters, Phoebe and Sylvia Ann, trav-

eled to Washington to take up the family cause. Clay and Webster supported their suit, and they sought the support of John Quincy Adams. The last words written by Mr. Adams were, "Mr. J. Q. Adams presents his compliments to the Misses Wood, and will be happy to see them at his house, at their convenience, any morning between 10 and 11 o'clock."

The note was found on February 21, 1848, the day that he had a stroke and died at his desk in the House of Representatives after saying, "This is the last of earth; I am content." The legislation, containing the words, "a bill providing that in these four heirs should rest for seven years the exclusive right of making and vending the improvements in the construction of the cast iron plow; and that twenty-five cents on each plow might be extracted from all who manufactured it," passed in the Senate but was defeated in the House of Representatives.

Competing plow manufacturers had convinced their representatives in Congress that the Wood family had gained considerable wealth from Jethro Wood's design in the previous twenty-eight years, and that they merely wanted to maintain the monopoly. It was estimated that royalties totaling $550 had been received by the family by 1834, the year in which Jethro Wood died. This sum didn't even cover legal costs.

Lobbying by the plow manufacturers included the exchange of money. At one point, Sylvia Ann Wood was told, privately, by the chairman of the committee considering the patent extension, that a few thousand dollars would give her a favorable verdict. However, with her sheltered Quaker upbringing, she did not understand what was being asked.

There were no teeth in the patent legislation of the time, and similar fates were suffered by other inventors, notably Charles Goodyear, inventor of the vulcanization process for rubber, and Eli Whitney, inventor of the cotton gin. Eli Whitney's experience in a Georgia court was typical: "I had great difficulty in proving that the machine had been used in Georgia, although at the same moment there were three separate sets of this machinery in motion within fifty yards of the building in which the court sat, and all so near that the rattling of wheels was distinctly heard on the steps of the Court House."

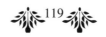

Scientific American magazine ranks Jethro Wood as an inventor with Benjamin Franklin, Robert Fulton, Charles Goodyear, Elias Howe, Cyrus McCormick, Samuel B. Morse, and Eli Whitney. William H. Seward, a counselor for the Wood family in their suit for royalties, observed that, "No citizen of the United States has conferred greater economical benefits on his country than Jethro Wood—none of her benefactors have been more inadequately rewarded."

The Origin of Lacrosse

Lacrosse originated with the North American Indians, who played the game long before the Europeans discovered America. Nicolas Perrot, an agent of the French government and a trader, provided one of the earliest descriptions of the game:

> The savages have a certain game of "cross" which is very similar to our tennis. They match tribe against tribe and if their number are not equal they withdraw some of the men from the stronger side. They are all armed with a "cross" stick which has a large portion laced with a racket. The ball with which they play is of wood and nearly the shape of a turkey's egg. It is the rule of the contest that after a side has won two goals, they change sides of the field with their opponents, and that two out of three or three out of five goals decide the game.

Native Americans played the game from the time that the ice melted until harvest time. The game was played by men, women, girls, and boys. Frequently, arms and legs were broken, and a crippling injury was not an infrequent occurence. Participants were even killed on occasion. Usually, players who were killed had been obstinate and refused to relinquish the ball. When this happened, the player's body was carried to his lodge in disgrace. Participants did not complain about injuries; they considered them to be part of the game.

French missionaries among the Hurons called the game "bagga-tie-way" or "le jeu de la crosse." Usually, 400 to 500 players were involved in a game pitting one village against another, but as many as 2,000 participants engaged in some of the games. When a famine or a serious epidemic occurred, the medicine men called for a game of lacrosse to appease the spirits. Most of the tribe participated, and ceremonies and religious dances were held when the game was over. Some members of the tribe were chosen to impersonate the evil spirits and to be punished. If some of the impersonators died, the spirits were appeased.

Lacrosse was played on all important occasions, particularly when entertaining guests. Rivalry between tribes was fierce. A championship game was an important event, and players fasted for the last day and night before the game. Prayers to the Great Spirit were offered for days leading up to the championship. Native Americans viewed the game as exercise to prepare their bodies for battle. They also considered it to be training in the tactics of attack and defense.

Stephen Powers commented on the game of lacrosse as played by the Pomas Indians in California, "They played it with a ball rounded out of an oak knot, propelled by a racket constructed of a long slender stick bent double and bound together leaving a circular hoop at the end, across which is woven a coarse mesh-work of strings. Such an instrument is not strong enough to bat the ball but simply to shove or thrust it along the ground."

Many variations of the game existed. Some tribes played with two goals about 150 feet apart. The Choctaws played with two lacrosse sticks but with only one goal; the goal was made of two poles that were approached from sixty yards away. The distance between the goals was 500 to 600 paces on some playing fields and up to one or one and a half miles on others. Eighty to a hundred players on a side was common. Many of the southern tribes played with two sticks between which the ball was caught. They were shorter than the single lacrosse sticks used by the northern tribes. The double sticks were usually about two feet long.

The Native Americans on the Pacific coast started the game by throwing a doeskin ball into the air. The ball was thrown by a maiden chosen for her beauty. Throwing the ball in a way that gave

one side the advantage was a serious offense. Even a maiden's beauty wouldn't protect her from punishment if she favored one side with her throw.

Considerable variety also existed in the players' clothing. Domench described one costume: "The players were costumed with short drawers, or rather a belt, the body being first daubed with a layer of bright colors. From the belt which is short enough to leave the thigh free, hangs a long animal tail. Round their necks is a necklace of animal's teeth to which is attached a floating mane dyed red, as is the tail, falling as a fringe over chest and shoulders."

Gradually, the game of lacrosse evolved. The large numbers on each side were reduced to fourteen or fifteen. The wooden ball was replaced by one made of scraped deerskin stuffed with deer hair and sewed with sinew. The early single bowed stick and the double sticks strapped together evolved to a single stick with strong netting. There has been considerable speculation about the first nation to play lacrosse. Many Native American nations claim to have originated the game, but the most convincing claim is that of the Iroquois Confederation of New York State.

 ### The Origin of Wampum

ccording to legend, when Da-ga-no-we-da, the peacemaker, approached the land of the Mohawks to attempt to bring peace to the five nations that were to become the Iroquois Confederacy, he crossed a lake believed to have been Oneida Lake. He saw many small purple and white shells sticking to the paddles of his canoe. As he approached the far side of the lake, he noticed piles of the shells along the shoreline. He filled some deerskin bags with the shells and, at his rest stops, strung the shells on deer sinews and then attached the strings together.

On the first wampum belt that he made, he used purple shells for the pictorial figures and white shells for the background. Five symbols representing the five nations were interwoven with five men clasping hands representing brotherly union. He created other belts that represented, for example, some law or council ceremony, death, war, peace, or civil proceedings, such as the installment of a chief. Purple shells were a sign of mourning and war, and white shells symbolized peace.

The wampum belts that were the symbols of law, Ote-ko-a, were woven of purple and white cylindrical beads about three sixteenths of an inch long. The purple beads were fashioned from the purple spot in the clam shell, and the white beads were made from the conch shell. Most of the older belts were strung on twisted threads from the inner bark of the elm tree. These strings were separated by strings of buckskin, with the belt joined together with fine threads of deer sinew.

Wampum beads, strung in lengths of four inches to a foot, were used as a message of peace or war. White beads were used in a "peace string;" a "war string" was made of purple beads. Belts of purple wampum were symbols of death, and if decorated with a red feather or red paint, signified war. These belts were used as ransom for a life or for multiple lives.

Councils were convened when a string of wampum was carried by a runner from nation to nation. Actions of a council were

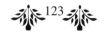

neither proposed nor ratified unless sealed by wampum, and a treaty wasn't considered valid until wampum belts had been exchanged.

One of the finest wampum belts in the possession of the Onondaga Nation is the "George Washington belt," which was exchanged at a peace treaty during Washington's presidency. It has 15 rows of 650 beads each, for a total of 9,750 beads. The symbol of a house with a gable roof and an open door is woven from white beads on a background of purple beads.

Men on both sides of the door, "guardians of the door," are depicted clasping hands with other men, six on one side and seven on the other side of the open door. The clasped hands signify unity or "the unbroken chain of friendship." The house represents the hall of the United States Government, and the open door connotes peace. The thirteen men clasping hands with the "keepers of the east and west doors" symbolize the thirteen colonies.

President Lincoln's Resident Artist

orn in Homer on August 6, 1830, Francis Bicknell Carpenter was a well-known and prolific artist. He became famous for his painting, *The First Reading of the Emancipation Proclamation,* which depicted President Lincoln and his cabinet: Attorney General Edward Bates, Postmaster-General Montgomery Blair, Secretary of Treasury Salmon Chase, Secretary of State William Seward, Secretary of the Interior Caleb Smith, Secretary of War Edwin Stanton, and Secretary of Navy Gideon Welles.

Carpenter was the second child of Asaph Carpenter and Almira Clark Carpenter. He displayed an interest in art early in his life on the farm, where he sketched many farm scenes in account books. In his mid-teens, he studied with Sanford Thayer in Syracuse and returned to establish a studio in Homer. By 1851, he realized that the next step in his development was to study with artists in New York City.

One of Carpenter's early commissions in New York was the painting of a portrait of President Millard Fillmore. His success with this painting brought him recognition, and he was asked to paint a portrait of Fillmore's successor, President Franklin Pierce. Carpenter spent part of 1855 in Washington, D.C., painting portraits of ex-President John Tyler and Senator Seward. Later, he painted a portrait of President John A. Garfield.

With the outbreak of the Civil War in 1861, Carpenter became a supporter of the Union war effort and a strong antislavery advocate. After the signing of the Emancipation Proclamation in 1863, Carpenter was moved by a desire to capture on canvas President Lincoln's reading of the proclamation to his Cabinet. Unfortunately, Carpenter had no contacts in the White House who could put forward his proposal. Finally, he decided to work though Illinois congressman Owen Lovejoy.

On January 5, 1863, Carpenter wrote Lovejoy about his suggestion:

> It is to paint a picture of one of the greatest subjects for a historical picture ever presented to an artist, *President Lincoln Reading the Proclamation of Independence* [sic] to his Cabinet, previous to its publication. I have been studying the design of the picture for several weeks and I never felt a stronger conviction or asssurance in any undertaking in my life! ... I wish to paint this picture now while all the actors in the scene are living and while they are still in the discharge of their duties of their several high offices. I wish to make it the standard authority for the portrait of each and all, particularly Mr. Lincoln....

Congressman Lovejoy provided the necessary introduction to the White House, and Carpenter received financial backing to do the painting from Frederick A. Lane. On February 4, 1864, the artist traveled to Washington to attend a reception at the White House to meet the President:

> Two o'clock found me pressing toward the center of attraction, the "blue" room. From the threshold of the "crimson" parlor as I passed, I had a glimpse of the gaunt

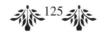

figure of Mr. Lincoln in the distance, haggard looking, dressed in black, relieved only by the prescribed white gloves; standing, it seemed to me, solitary and alone, although surrounded by the crowd, bending low now and then in the process of hand-shaking, and responding half abstractedly to the well-meant greetings.

Carpenter moved along in the reception line and was introduced to the President, who shook his hand and said, "Oh yes ... this is the painter. Do you think, Mr. Carpenter, that you can make a handsome picture of me?" Carpenter met with the President in his office later that day. Lincoln read Congressman Lovejoy's letter of introduction and commented, "Well, Mr. Carpenter, we will turn you loose here, and try to give you a good chance to work out your idea."

Carpenter moved into the White House in mid-February and, for the next six months, painted and observed Lincoln and his staff at work during the last year of the Civil War. He did most of his painting in the state dining room, but he did his preliminary sketches in the cabinet room, where one visitor asked about Carpenter's presence. Lincoln responded, "You need not mind him, he is but a painter." The artist was a Lincoln supporter when he moved into the Presidential mansion, but, after seeing the President at work, he became an admirer.

Carpenter took advantage of the new technology of photography to assist him with his painting. He invited one of Civil War photographer Matthew Brady's cameramen to the White House to take photographs to supplement his preliminary sketches. Carpenter finished his work in July and sought the President's opinion. Lincoln looked at the nine-foot by fifteen-foot canvas and commented that the characterizations had been done as well as they could have been. The President thought that the visualization of himself and his cabinet was "absolutely perfect."

Carpenter returned to New York City, where he was inundated with requests for paintings. In 1866, he commissioned an engraver, Alexander Hay Ritchie, to make copies of the Emancipation Proclamation painting. Ritchie commented, "For several months after the plate was finished, the orders could only be supplied by printing from the plate night and day.... Nearly 30,000 impressions were printed from the steel plate, which is now worn out."

Carpenter wrote a book about his stay in the Presidential mansion, *Six Months at the White House with Abraham Lincoln*. The book went through sixteen editions and provided a comfortable income for the painter, although he himself thought that his book was "rambling and fragmentary."

Carpenter's book was the only source of many stories about Lincoln. Carpenter told of a clergyman who expressed the hope to Lincoln that the Lord was on "our side." Putting things in their proper perspective, Lincoln responded with the hope "that this nation should be on the Lord's side." The painter / author also captured Lincoln's strong wish that every Wall Street gold speculator should have "his devilish head shot off."

He also did portraits of Grant's Vice President, Schuyler Colfax, and of John C. Fremont, U.S. Senator from California, presidential candidate, and governor of the Arizona Territory. Carpenter also painted portraits of Horace Greeley of the New York *Tribune*, Henry Jarvis Raymond of the New York *Times*, U.S. Senator Charles Sumner, and Daniel Webster.

Carpenter's reputation continued to grow. *International Arbitration*, his painting of the signing of the Treaty of Washington by Great Britain and the United States, was purchased for the private collection of Queen Victoria. Carpenter painted a total of sixteen portraits of Lincoln.

In 1878, Carpenter sold the *First Reading of the Emancipation Proclamation* to Elizabeth Thompson, who donated it to the U.S. government. Today, it hangs in the U.S. Capitol. Reporter Noah Brooks called the painting, "a picture which will be prized in every liberty-loving household as a work of art, a group of faithful likenesses of the President and his Cabinet, and as a perpetual remembrance of the noblest event in American history."

The Story of the Franklin Automobile

 erbert Henry Franklin, owner of a die-casting company, and John Wilkinson, designer of a "horseless carriage," met in 1901. In 1903, Franklin opened an automobile plant on South Geddes Street in Syracuse to produce automobiles to Wilkinson's design. The first model was a two-passenger car with a valve-in-head four-cylinder air-cooled engine. The first car off the line cost $1,000 and had a top speed of thirty miles per hour. The advantages of the air-cooled engine were the elimination of the radiator and a reduction in the weight of the car.

In 1906, the Franklin automobile ranked third in sales of all cars manufactured in the United States. By 1916, the H. H. Franklin Manufacturing Company had 2,300 employees and produced 15,000 cars per year. In the late 1920s the company had eighteen buildings with thirty-four acres of floor space on sixteen acres of land. Franklin automobiles were known for their quality engineering and their dependability. Included in Franklin's innovations were:

- first six-cylinder engine (1905)
- first drive-through springs and transmission service brakes (1906)
- first use of automatic spark advance (1907)
- first use of aluminum pistons (1911)
- first exhaust jackets for heating intake gases
- first closed bodies and sedans

Franklin designed a transmission for U.S. Army tanks in World War I. The company also produced parts for airplane motors, for depth charges, and for the Curtiss biplane during the first World War. By 1929, the H. H. Franklin Manufacturing Company had 3,200 employees and was the largest employer of skilled labor in the Syracuse area. However, as the Great Depression progressed, the company struggled with financial difficulties. No one could afford to buy their fine cars. After experiencing significant losses, the company filed for bankruptcy and closed in 1934.

Chapter 13

Eclectic / Extraordinary Stories

 **Buffalo Bill's Rochester Connection**

illiam Frederick "Buffalo Bill" Cody was an army scout, a buffalo hunter, an Indian fighter, and a Wild West Show performer. The Cody family moved to Rochester in 1874 and resided at 434 Exchange Street. They lived briefly at the Waverly Hotel on State Street and then moved to 10 New York Street, off Jefferson Avenue.

Buffalo Bill was tall and broad-shouldered, with long, black, curly hair and a well-trimmed goatee and mustache. He smoked cigars and wore a wide-brimmed hat and a black coat with tails. A gold watch chain with large links hung across the front of his vest. He was an extroverted, minimally-educated product of the frontier.

Cody was born on February 26, 1846, in LeClair, Iowa. At the age of twelve, he killed his first Indian—to foil an attack on a wagon train. During the Civil War, he fought as a "Jayhawk" with a guerrilla band in Kansas. He joined the Union Army as a scout and was promoted to captain. In 1865, he married Louise Fredereci of St. Louis.

After the war, Cody became a U.S. Cavalry scout in campaigns against the Native Americans. The Indians called him "Pahaska," the long-haired one. He left the army and became a hunter, a pony express rider, a stage coach driver, a trapper, a wagon master, and a wagon train courier. He became known as "Buffalo Bill" after he killed 4,280 buffaloes in a year and a half to furnish meat for the men building the Kansas Pacific Railroad. Also, he operated as a guide on buffalo hunts for celebrities, such as General Philip Sheridan, the Grand Duke Alexis of

Russia, and James Gordon Bennett, the New York publisher.

Edward Judson, using the pseudonym Ned Buntline, placed Buffalo Bill before the American public and made him famous. Judson wrote hundreds of stories in which Buffalo Bill was the hero. Cody's popularity, particularly in the East, encouraged him to go on the stage. Bill's first thespian effort was *The Scout of the Plains* in Chicago. The play was poorly written and the acting matched the quality of the play, but there was considerable action and shooting. The audience loved it. Later the cast included Kit Carson, Jr., Bill's friend Texas Jack, and Wild Bill Hickock.

By 1874, Cody had decided that a traveling company was not a good environment for his wife and three young children, so he moved his family to Rochester. In 1875, Buffalo Bill starred at the Grand Opera House, later the Embassy, in his new home city. By that time, Native Americans had joined the cast. When they weren't on the stage, Bill and his crony, Texas Jack, sat in Main Street saloons in their western outfits and told stories of the Wild West.

Arta and Kit, the two oldest Cody children, attended School No. 2 on King Street. The school principal was Mary S. Anthony, Susan B. Anthony's sister. In April, 1876, both Arta and Kit contracted scarlet fever. Cody, who was performing in Boston at the time, received a telegram from Louise requesting him to come home. He arrived just before Kit died. Much of the light in Bill's life went out when Kit, his only son, was buried in Mt. Hope Cemetery.

Cody tired of life on the stage and rejoined the U.S. Cavalry as chief of scouts. He moved his family to Nebraska except for Arta, who stayed behind in Rochester to study at the Livingston Park Academy in the Third Ward. Bill was motivated to join the army because the Sioux were stirring up unrest in the Dakotas. The feelings of the country were elevated by the massacre of General George Armstrong Custer and his men at Little Big Horn. Bill gained some notoriety by killing the Sioux chief, Yellow Hand, in a duel.

At the conclusion of the Sioux wars, Bill went back on the stage—for the remainder of his life. Annie Oakley co-starred with Bill in his new show. They performed for Queen Victoria in England, where Bill became a companion of Edward, the Prince of

Wales. During Queen Victoria's Golden Jubilee, Cody and the Prince of Wales gave the Kings of Belgium, Denmark, and Greece a wild ride at breakneck speed through London in Bill's Deadwood coach, while being chased by whooping and hollering Indians on horseback.

In 1883, Cody and his wife returned to Rochester to bury their eleven-year-old daughter, Orra, next to her brother in Mt. Hope cemetery. Bill's Wild West show returned to Rochester every year to give a performance. In 1904, Bill and Louise returned to Rochester to inter their oldest daughter, Arta, alongside her brother and sister. She died at the age of thirty-eight, just three weeks before she was to marry an army surgeon.

Cody did not manage his finances well. He had to sell a half interest in his show to James C. Bailey, the Bailey of Barnum and Bailey. Eventually, Cody had to sell his remaining half of the show and go to work for the Sells Floto Circus.

Buffalo died in Denver in 1917 at the age of seventy-one. His fans viewed his body in the Colorado capitol before he was buried on Lookout Mountain. Bill was a legend in his own time and one of the last remnants of a wild frontier. He became a symbol of a West that had changed forever.

 ## The Discovery of a Mastodon Skeleton

n January, 1991, construction workers dug up the skull of a mastodon in a peat bog near Avon. The skull belonged to a mastodon that had roamed western New York 10,000 to 12,000 years ago during the Pleistocene epoch. Mastodons, ancestors of the elephant, were indigenous to the southern Great Lakes region until after the second Ice Age. Mastodons had large trunks, long, heavy limbs, and massive heads. American mastodons had two large tusks.

Scientists uncovered the entire skeleton, which survived intact where the animal died while lying on its side. The skeleton was

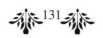

found about five feet below the surface in layers of peat and marl (earth, sand, and shells). Scientists estimate that the mastodon was about eight to nine feet tall at the shoulder. Mastodon bones have been found at other "digs," but finding a complete skeleton is rare. Scientists at the State University of New York—College at Geneseo guided the effort to preserve the skeleton intact.

The End of the World

In 1818, William Miller of Low Hampton, Washington County, New York, believed that the second coming of Jesus Christ was imminent. By 1832, when he was fifty years old, he concluded from an intrepretation of the scripture and from his own impressions that:

> The end of the world is at hand. The evidence flows in from every quarter. The earth is reeling to and fro like a

132

drunkard.... See the carnivorous fowls fly screaming
through the air! See—see these signs! Behold the heavens
grow black with clouds; the sun has veiled himself; the
moon, pale and forsaken, hangs in the middle air; the hail
descends, the seven thunders utter loud their voices; the
lightnings send their vivid gleams of sulphurous flames
abroad; and the great city of nations falls to rise no more
forever and forever. At this dread moment, look! The
clouds have burst asunder; the heavens appear, the great
white throne is in sight! ... He comes! Behold the savior
comes!

At first, no one listened to Miller's predictions of doom. Then,
a year after his first prediction, many shooting stars felt to the
earth. The event was perceived as a omen. Across the northern
skies, a bright shooting star with a large, flaming tail seemed to
provide a second sign. Miller said, "Ten years from now, the Christ
will appear a second time in the clouds of heaven. He will raise the
righteous dead and judge them with the righteous living who will
be caught up to meet him in the air. The earth will be sacrificed by
fire and the wicked and all their works will be consumed."

Miller, a Baptist who was a student of Old Testament prophe-
cies, concluded that the 2,300 days of Daniel in 8:14 really meant
2,300 years, and that the countdown had begun with Ezra's journey
to Jerusalem in BC 457. Therefore, the end of the world would
occur in 1843.

Specifically, as related by Carl Carmer in *Listen for a
Lonesome Drum*:

Considering each day mentioned in Biblical prophecy as a
year, William Miller's preliminary figuring brought him to the
number 2,300 from which he was able to make other significant calculations. Here is his first calculation:

From the date of the commandment to rebuild
Jerusalem, BC 457 to the crucifixion of
Christ, 70 weeks, or 490 years   490

From the crucifixion of Christ to taking away the daily abomination of which is supposed to signify Paganism	475
From taking away of Pagan rites to setting up the abomination of desolation, or Papal Civil Rule	30
From setting up the Papal abomination to the end thereof	1,260
From taking away of Papal Civil Rule to the first resurrection and the End of the World in 1843	45
These being added present the sum of the years	2,300

Subtracting from 2,300 the seventy weeks of years, 490, up to the crucifixion of Christ and adding the resultant figure to the years of the Savior's life, 33, gives the date of the end of the world as 1843 AD.

Or merely subtracting from the 2300 previously arrived at the date of the commandment to rebuild Jerusalem, BC 457, at once gives the date to the end of the world—1843.

Or simply add to the second item of the first calculation above, 475, the number of years in the Savior's life plus Daniel's number, 1,335, and the date of the end of the world is 1843.

Miller's ideas began to attract widespread attention. Churches opened their doors to him. He lectured widely in the Midwest and the East, including central and western New York. Miller announced that April 21, 1843, was the date for which he had been preparing people. Many farmers didn't prepare fields for crops that spring because they wouldn't be around to plant, tend, and harvest them. Many businessmen abandoned their businesses, and many people gave away all of their possessions.

When the designated day came and went, Miller's followers didn't know what to believe. Miller announced that he had made a

mistake in the calculations because he had used the Hebrew calendar instead of the Roman calendar. His new calculations indicated that October 22, 1844, was the correct date for the end of the world.

On the night of October 22, Miller's righteous followers put on their white robes and climbed onto roofs and into trees to await their ascension while the non-righteous perished in flames on earth. In Rochester, many Millerites climbed Cobb's Hill to look upward toward the heavens, knowing that morning would never come. When the sun came up in the East, as usual, many disillusioned people returned to their homes.

On November 6, 1844, Miller made an appeal in the Rochester *Daily Advertiser* for those of his followers who had not given away their worldly possessions to share them with those who had. He pleaded with his followers not to let their brethren appeal for charity. He was concerned that the members of other churches would scoff at them.

In 1845, Miller and those of his followers who remained with him and still believed in the Advent met in Albany and formed an Adventist organization. Subsequently, this organization split into several groups. One group of Adventists in western New York joined the Seventh-Day Baptists of Maine and moved on with the pioneers to the Midwest. Another of the splinter groups became the Seventh-Day Adventists, who observe the Sabbath on Saturday instead of Sunday.

How a British Subject Became President of the United States

hester A. Arthur, the twenty-first President of the United States, spent five of his formative years—from age ten to age fifteen— in the Finger Lakes Region. He lived in Perry from 1835 to 1837 and in York from 1837 to 1839. Chester A. Arthur, elected Vice President in 1880, became President upon the death of President James Garfield on September 19, 1881.

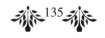

A story circulated in 1880 and 1881 that Arthur had been born in Canada and therefore was not eligible to become Vice President or President of the United States. A New York attorney, Arthur P. Hinman, was the source of the rumor. In 1884, Hinman published a book, *How a British Subject Became the President of the United States*, in which he attempted to prove that Arthur had been born in Canada.

Hinman asserted that William Arthur and Malvina Stone Arthur had three sons: William Chester Alan Arthur, supposedly born in Dunham, Quebec; Chester Abell Arthur, born in Fairfield, Vermont; and William Arthur, Jr., born in Hinesburgh, Vermont. When William Arthur, Jr., was born, the oldest son dropped the William from his name. He could do this without confusion because his younger brother, Chester Abell Arthur, had died in infancy.

Hinman claimed that President Arthur appropriated the birth certificate of his younger brother, Chester Abell Arthur. Furthermore, there was no death record for Chester Abell because their father, William Arthur, had sold his infant son's body to a medical school. Therefore, the substitution could not be proved. Hinman alleged that Chester A. Arthur was a British subject, and therefore was ineligible to be elected Vice President or to be elevated to the Presidency upon the death of President Garfield.

The New York *Sun* investigated Hinman's claims and refuted the story on the day after Arthur was sworn in as President. His ancestry was clearly understood by the public as he began his duties as the twenty-first President of the United States. In spite of Hinman's extensive assertions, his politically motivated ruse was ineffective.

The Improvisation

The Eastman Theater in Rochester was built in 1921-22 and opened on September 4, 1922. The main chandelier that is suspended over the orchestra section was installed in time for the opening performance, but the two small chandeliers for the balcony section did not arrive. A quick decision was made to buy two galvanized laundry tubs, paint them, and decorate them to look like small chandeliers. The action was intended as a stopgap measure until the chandeliers on order were received.

The two small chandeliers were never delivered, and the two decorated laundry tubs became permanent fixtures. In 1971, when the Eastman Theater was restored to its original condition, a decision was made to replace the laundry tubs with real chandeliers. However, those committee members who knew the story of the tubs indulged themselves in some nostalgia and voted to keep them in place. They prevailed, and the inverted tubs are still there as surrogate chandeliers.

The Mysterious Ruin North of Branchport

n addition to the ruins reminiscent of Stonehenge on the bluff of Keuka Lake, a second set of ruins existed within the town of Jerusalem. It was located in the northwestern corner of Jerusalem in the hamlet of Friend, also called "Old Fort," about one mile west of the home of the Jemima Wilkinson, the Publick Universal Friend. Jemima's house is located on Friend Hill Road, off Friend Road.

The "Old Fort" was described in 1880 by Dr. Samuel Hart Wright, MD, who was an internationally known biologist and a surveyor:

> An aboriginal earthwork in Jerusalem known as the "Old Fort," we find by well recognized works and pointed out by the oldest inhabitants of the locality, is an ellipse having 545 feet transverse diameter from north to south and 485 feet conjugate diameter from east to west. The outside was a raised earthwork, having twelve gateways nearly equally distributed around, the narrower being eight feet wide and alternating with the wider ones about fourteen

feet wide. A deep, wide trench ran around the work. The enclosure contained four and three-fourths acres, and there were two dwelling houses and a school house on this ground. (Later a church has been erected upon the site.)

A large opening in the enclosure about fifty feet east of the spring was seventy feet wide, and in front or west of which is a steep bank of coarse gravel, into which a bay has been dug out by a large spring which is about eight to ten feet below the edge of the bank. The land east and north of the spring is a series of extensive sand banks, the aboriginal enclosure itself being a low bank and rising everywhere to the center.

We found fragments of Indian pottery in a large quantity of old ashes nearby, in which was also found recently, by the owner of the land, a broken bowl of a pipe made of baked clay. A French gun lock was also found.

In the recollection of many persons these grounds were covered with a dense forest of pines, and an old stump of old oak nearly four feet in diameter now stands on the edge of the embankment.

Many years ago a Seneca chief told Bartleson Sherman that his Nation knew nothing of the origin of the work, and that it was there when his people first knew of this land.

We surveyed and mapped this work for the Smithsonian Institution on the 28th of July, 1880.

SAMUEL HART WRIGHT

An unusual fact about this site is that it was built in a region of sandy loam with no stones in the the immediate area. A kneading board made of fine, compact sandstone was discovered by an early settler on the site of the ruin. The stone was two and a half inches thick with a slightly concave surface. The artifact was made of dif-

ferent material than any geological formation in the region. It was similar to kneading boards used by the Indians in Mexico.

It appears that specimens of ancient pottery found on the site were made by a civilized people with knowledge different from that of the Iroquois Indians in the area. The ruins at "Old Fort" also appear to predate the entrance of the Iroquois to the region.

"Red Emma" Goldman of Rochester

E mma Goldman was born in 1869 in Kovno, Russia. In 1882, the Goldman family moved to St. Petersburg, where Emma worked as a seamstress in a glove factory. She had an unhappy home life. Her mother was cold to her; the family's favorite was Emma's older half sister, Helena. Her autocratic father was bitter because of his business failures. An older sister, Lena, had emigrated to the United States, married, and was living in Rochester. In 1885, Emma and Helena joined their sister, Lena.

Emma worked as a seamstress making overcoats ten and a half hours a day for $2.50 a week. She asked her boss for a raise so that she could buy books and theater tickets as she had in St. Petersburg. He refused and told her that her thoughts were too fancy for a worker in a clothing factory. She quit that job and got a job in a smaller factory for $4.00 for a six-day week. Emma was disillusioned with life in the land of the free.

In 1886, Emma's parents and two brothers joined the sisters in Rochester. They lived in an apartment on Joseph Avenue. A boarder, Jacob Kirshner, lived with the family. Emma and Jacob were married when she was seventeen, but they were divorced within a year.

In her 1931 autobiography, *Living My Life*, Emma wrote about finding "an escape from the gray dullness of Rochester existence" in the weekly Socialist meetings in Germania Hall. At a meeting of the Socialist group, she heard of the Chicago Haymarket bombing. Six extremists were sentenced to death without proof of their guilt.

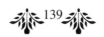

Emma was deeply moved by the injustice of the incident. It drove her to read anarchist literature and to become a staunch anarchist. She began to participate in the activities of the far left wing in the class war.

Emma realized that she could be more active in left wing activities if she lived in New York. Also, New York offered many more cultural activities than did Rochester. In August, 1889, with $5.00 in her handbag, a sewing machine, and some clothing, she arrived in the big city. She brought along her intense hatred of capitalist society's institutions. She was welcomed heartily into anarchist groups, where she met Alexander Berkman, a fiery liberal, and Johann Most, a radical editor. Both were to influence her life as an extremist.

Most helped her to improve her speaking style. She became an intense speaker who effectively projected her beliefs. She went on a lecture tour to speak on the behalf of the Haymarket prisoners. She spoke at the German Union in Rochester, where she was vocal about the city's clothing "sweat shops."

Emma declared that she believed in "free love." At one point in her life, she shared rooms with two lovers, Berkman and a young artist, at the same time. In 1892, Berkman traveled to Pittsburgh to kill Henry Frick, who led the attack against the strikers at the Homestead Works of the Carnegie Steel Company. Berkman stabbed Frick once and shot him three times, but he didn't succeed in killing him. Berkman, who was captured in Frick's office with a stick of dynamite in his mouth, received a twenty-two-year prison sentence and served sixteen years of the sentence.

After completing nurses' training, Emma worked as a nurse and continued with her radical activites. She was the editor of the radical publication, *Mother Earth*, until the government shut it down during World War I. She lectured widely. Frequently, she was billed as lecturing on drama, a subject that she knew well, but she managed to convey her political viewpoints interwoven with the discussion of drama. In 1893, she was convicted of inciting a riot in Union Square and served a year in jail on Blackwell's Island. She ran the jail's infirmary while serving her sentence.

Emma was in St. Louis when she heard of the shooting of President McKinley in Buffalo. She saw a newspaper containing a picture of his assassin, Leon Czolgosz, and the headline, "Emma Goldman Sought." She recognized Czolgosz as the young extremist, Fred Nieman, with whom she had talked in Cleveland. However, they didn't talk about McKinley, and Emma had nothing to do with the assassination.

Czolgosz told the police that he knew Emma, thus triggering a search for her. The police searched the homes of her relatives in Rochester. She traveled from St. Louis to Chicago, where she was taken into custody. She was interrogated in jail for several days, where she claimed that she was beaten before being released. Although she was cleared from any participation in the shooting of President McKinley, she was associated with it in the public's mind. She later claimed that she was suspected in participating of every act of violence in the United States after 1901.

Emma was definitely a free spirit. She advocated atheism, free love, and the overthrow of the government. She spent fifteen days in the workhouse for promoting birth control. She smoked two packs of cigarettes a day at a time when few women smoked. She and Berkman advocated resisting the draft during World War I and were both jailed for two years. Upon their release from prison in September 1919, they were deported to Russia along with 250 other Socialists and Communists.

Emma looked forward to living in Communist Russia, but she became more disillusioned there than she had been in America.

The distrust, oppression, and terror under the new Communist government were no better than conditions under the Czars. After two years, she left Russia for Sweden and then Germany. She lectured in England and France about the shortcomings of the Russian experience. She married a Welsh miner, James Colton, to obtain British citizenship to ease her entrance to Canada.

While she lived in Canada, President Roosevelt approved a ninety-day visa for her to visit the United States. She spoke to the City Club forum in Rochester, a decidedly conservative forum, and told them, "I am no more respectable than I ever was. It is you who are a little more liberal. Your city and the action of the State of Illinois in the Haymarket cases made an anarchist out of me." She died in Toronto in 1940 at the age of seventy. She had rebelled against traditional beliefs until her final breath.

The Story of Bill—Version I

William Avery Rockefeller, the father of John D. Rockefeller, moved to Richford, Tioga County, in 1834, when he was in his early twenties. William, known as "Big Bill," was just over six foot tall, barrel-chested, and broad-shouldered, with deep-set calculating eyes and an auburn beard. He liked to tell stories and had a ready wit. Big Bill was quick to laugh and was known as a ladies' man. He was also an accomplished horseback rider and a crack shot with a rifle.

Big Bill did not drink but occasionally bought a round of drinks for his friends. He did not like farming; he engaged in many activities that caused him to be frequently away from home, including buying and selling horses and selling housewares and patent medicine from a wagon. When he visited Iroquois reservations, he pretended to be deaf and dumb because he thought that the Native Americans considered this to be a sign of power.

On one of his selling trips, Bill stopped at the Davison household in Moravia and met twenty-three-year-old Eliza Davison. When he knocked at the door to the house he held out a small blackboard and a piece of chalk to use in communicating. Later, Eliza said, "If that man were not deaf and dumb, I'd marry him." He wasn't, and she did.

On February 26, 1837, Bill and Eliza were married and moved to Richford, near his parents. Bill bought a one and a half story frame house on sixty acres on Michigan Hill, four miles northeast of the village of Richford. The first three Rockefeller children were born there: Lucy, John D., and William, Jr. In 1843, they moved to Moravia, Cayuga County, near the homestead of Eliza's family. Big Bill, who always seemed to have ready money, made a $1,000 down payment on the seven-room white frame farmhouse and paid off the $2,100 mortgage within a few years.

While they lived in Moravia, many stories circulated about the mysterious activities of William Avery Rockefeller. Neighbors heard horses neighing and lanterns glowing at night. People talked about a cave at the end of a gully reached by a secret path. The natives heard about a "horse underground" that operated between the Finger Lakes Region and the South, particularly Maryland and Virginia. Initially, horses from Virginia appeared for sale in Upstate New York, and later there were rumors of New York State horses being sold in the South.

Ultimately, vigilante committees were formed to break up the gangs of horse thieves. In 1850, three of Big Bill's cronies were indicted for horse stealing. On July 23, 1849, an indictment was recorded against Big Bill in the Cayuga County Courthouse. A page is missing from the records in the case at the Courthouse in Auburn. He was never brought to trial, and no record of the final disposition of the case exists. In 1850, the Rockefeller family moved to Owego, and three years later left the Finger Lakes Region to move to Cleveland, where later John D. Rockefeller made his fortune.

 ## The Story of Bill—Version II

his story is based on "The Tale of Old Bill" in *Listen for a Lonesome Drum* by Carl Carmer. Old Bill pretended to be deaf and dumb when he moved to Tompkins County. He drove a horse-drawn wagon loaded with patent medicines and housewares, and business was good. Few of the country and village women could resist the tall, powerfully-built man with the shining blue eyes. They felt sorry for him with his affliction.

Old Bill was impressed with Moravia in his travels and decided to buy a house there. He grew a beard and, eventually, let people forget that he was deaf and dumb. In fact, they learned that he would talk their ear off, particularly when he started on the evils of demon drink.

The townsfolk of Moravia liked Bill. He told amusing stories and was a good marksman. He attracted customers to his patent medicine wagon by placing a pipe in the mouth of a dummy and shattering the pipe with a bullet from 200 paces away. On one occasion at the Cortland County Fair, on an impulse, he altered his aim and shot the pipe out of the mouth of a startled bystander. Everyone who saw the incident was impressed with Old Bill's markmanship, except the man with the pipe. Bill gave him ten dollars for a new pipe, but the man was still angry.

Many residents of Dryden, McGraw, and Moravia had horses stolen during the middle of the night. Soon, area residents began to suspect Old Bill. They were aware that he frequently took extended trips, and they saw lights at night in the gully near his home. None of those who had their horses stolen ever saw their animals again. However, they did notice, particularly on the less-traveled roads, Bill's young helpers encouraging herds of horses to move along.

Eventually, the word got around that Old Bill had good Virginia horses to sell to Cayuga, Cortland, and Tompkins County farmers who had had their horses stolen. Area farmers also heard that many good New York State horses were being sold in Virginia.

Adverse feelings began to grow about Bill, but no one could prove anything. A young farmer spied on the suspected horse thief, but Bill caught him and kept him in a cave overnight. The horse thieves stepped up their activity.

Bill was taken to court in Auburn, where he attempted to make the jury believe that the young man who spied on him was the culprit. One of Bill's cronies in the witness box admitted that Bill was stealing horses. The jury, forgetting that they were in a court of law, vaulted the rail of the jury box and went after Bill. He climbed out of the window before they could reach him.

The people of Auburn were treated to seeing a man over six foot tall outracing a group of twelve men in pursuit. The men of the jury chased Bill over the county line, and he never returned to Cayuga County. Is this story fact or fiction? Readers can draw their own conclusions.

Chapter 14

Sources / Sites

Cobblestone Country

obblestone houses are indigenous to the Finger Lakes Region and the area just to the west of it. Homes constructed of cobblestones can be found within a fifty-mile radius of Rochester but, in significant numbers, nowhere else. Albany, Michigan, Ohio, and Ontario, Canada, each have a few examples of this type of architecture and Brattleboro, Vermont, has one. However, these homes were built by masons who moved there from central and western New York State. Among the inherent advantages of building a house with cobblestones are fire- and weather-resistance and low maintenance.

Cobblestones are water-washed stones that were produced by glacial activity during the Ice Age. As the glacier advanced, it ground and smoothed the stones and distributed them along the shoreline of Lake Iroquois, the region's glacial lake. Many the cobblestones were strewn along the "Ridge," now Ridge Road. Farmers removed the stones from their fields and piled them out of the way of their plows or made fences with them.

Cobblestone architecture is considered a regional expression of the architecture of the late Greek Revival Period, but it is not a separate style. Although the Greek Revival style began in the 1790s, the earliest cobblestone homes were built in the mid-1820s. Cobblestone architecture is divided into three periods: the Early Period (1825-1835), the Middle Period (1835-1845), and the Late Period (1845-1861). With few exceptions, the Cobblestone Era ended with the beginning of the Civil War.

Although most of the cobblestone homes were built in the Greek Revival style, some were built in the Post-

Colonial Style, and a few were built in the Victorian Style—the Civil War took place during the Victorian Period. Many of them were of a transitional design and had the characteristics of more than one style. The first cobblestone homes were built in Henrietta, Mendon, and Rush in Monroe County and in Farmington in Ontario County. Cobblestone houses were initially built on farms; later they appeared in the villages.

Stones used in the early cobblestone construction varied considerably in size and were laid in uneven rows. One of the first stylistic innovations was to lay the stones in more even rows. During the Early Period, the stones were from two and a half to three and a half inches high and from three to six inches long. Stones were sized by passing them through holes cut in a board or through iron rings called "beetle rings."

Smaller stones, from one and a half to two and a half inches high and from two to four inches long, were used during the Middle Period. Also, masons began to use stones of one particular color. Red sandstones were popular during this period.

Small round stones, called lake-washed cobblestones, were used widely during the Late Period. On the average, they were one to one and a half inches high and three-quarters of an inch to two inches wide. The herring-bone pattern was one of the variations used in the construction of cobblestone houses. The use of alternate rows of white and red stones was another.

From the beginning, masons used stone quoins at the corners of the houses. Quoins are rectangular stones used to strengthen corners and to improve the appearance of the building. Initially, these were small stone blocks about two or three courses of cobblestones high. Later, they used square stones twelve inches high, six to eight inches thick, and sixteen to eighteen inches long. As the size of the stones selected became smaller, four courses, then five courses, and, finally, six courses of stones were finished with a twelve-inch-high quoin at the corners.

It was not a coincidence that cobblestone houses began to be constructed in the mid-1820s. The Erie Canal was completed in 1825, and masons who built the locks on the canal were looking for work. They wanted to stay in the area because they liked the beauty of the region and the reasonable cost of land. The availability of

The Captain Throop house in Pultneyville

labor combined with the availability of material served to promote a new type of regional construction. This was particularly noticeable along the Ridge to the west of Rochester. There are over twenty-five examples of cobblestone architecture in the twenty-five-mile stretch between Rochester and the village of Childs.

Limestone blocks and slabs for quoins, sills, and lintels could be easily and economically transported from area quarries. A sill is the horizontal piece at the bottom of a door or window opening; a lintel is the horizontal piece over a door or window that bears the weight of the structure above it. During the construction of the Erie Canal, quarries had been established at Albion, Geneva, LeRoy, Medina, Phelps, and Rochester.

Not only homes, but also churches, schools, and stores were constructed of cobblestones. In addition, an octagonal blacksmith shop in Alloway, a factory in Perry, and a Masonic Temple Building in Pittsford were built of cobblestones. In all, approximately 500 cobblestone structures were erected in the region.

Interest in cobblestone structures tapered off as labor costs increased. Cobblestone construction was very labor-intensive, and also the advent of steam-powered sawmills and the availability of wood from Pennsylvania and from the Adirondacks lowered the cost of construction with wood.

Although some of the cobblestone houses have been lost, most of their owners today appear to be maintaining them properly. They certainly are worthy of being preserved. Rochester architect Claude Bragdon referred to the Cobblestone Era as "evidence of our architectural Golden Age." In his opinion, "Austere and humble as these buildings are, they show a beauty and integrity of a kind which made this country great, and should serve as inspiration to us today."

 ## The Origin of the Genesee River

he Genesee River, the only river that crosses the entire width of New York State, is one of the few major rivers that flows north. It meanders for approximately 190 miles from its origins in spring-fed ponds in Gold, Pennsylvania. The source of the Genesee River is in Potter County, Pennsylvania, near the headwaters of the Allegheny River and a branch of the Susquehanna River. The Iroquois Indians considered the river and its valley together when they named the river Genesee, meaning "beautiful valley."

The sea covered the Genesee Valley, as it covered the adjacent Finger Lakes Region, until 350 to 400 million years ago during the Devonian Period. When the sea receded from the valley, it left layers of mud, sand, and silt, which now can be seen as compressed layers in the Letchworth State Park gorge. An extended period of erosion and weathering followed the Devonian Era. In the hardrock layers, it created broad escarpments such as those south of Dansville, and formed lowlands and stream valleys in the softer layers.

The character of the Genesee Valley and the Finger Lakes was created by cyclical glacial erosion and glacial deposits, a process which deepened the north-south valleys and filled the east-west valleys. The major changes to the Genesee River were in the areas of Letchworth State Park and Rochester. Glacial residue filled an older channel from Portageville to Sonyea, and a similar channel was filled in between Avon and Irondequoit Bay, the original mouth of the Genesee River.

The Genesee-Canaseraga Valley from Geneseo to Dansville was a large lake similar to the Finger Lakes. The rich, fertile farmland in that area today was underwater for much of its history. After the glacier in the region retreated about 13,000 years ago, it readvanced to within five miles north of Geneseo and filled in the valley near Ashantee with glacial debris that partially blocked the original outlet of the Genesee River.

With the withdrawal of the glacier in the Wisconsin Ice Age, the new Genesee River followed its original course from Pennsylvania to Portageville, where the old northeast pathway to Sonyea was now blocked by glacial deposits of the Portageville moraine. From here, the new Genesee River flowed north across the Letchworth plateau, eventually eroding the plateau into the gorge that exists today. Similar erosion occurred at Rochester, when the new channel of the Genesee River to Lake Ontario was carved in rock older than that in Letchworth State Park.

The main geological features between Avon and Dansville are linked with the Genesee River, which meanders across a flat sediment-filled floor with "ox-bows," where the river doubles back on itself. The Dansville trough between Mt. Morris and Dansville now contains Caneseraga Creek. It was formed by the much larger "Dansville River," the east branch of the original Genesee River with headwaters near the present Canandaigua Lake.

The Origin of Rorick's Glen

Chiwenah, a beautiful Indian Maiden, was deeply in love with a young brave, Mintowan, of her tribe. They had grown up together, and she loved him for his compassionate nature, his strength, and his reputation for good judgment. However, Mintowan was in love with a young maiden from a neighboring tribe. When Mintowan married his loved one, Chiwenah was crushed. She sat in the doorway of her father's lodge and wept disconsolately.

She wept so hard and for so long that her tears began to form a furrow down the nearby hillside. Eventually, a spring pushed through the surface of the ground, and its waters joined with Chiwenah's tears. The furrow in the hillside grew deeper and deeper until it became the gorge that Elmirans know as Rorick's Glen.

The Origin of Rorick's Glen in Elmira

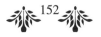

The Salt Industry in the Finger Lakes Region

Livingston County

he salt mine at Retsof in the town of York, owned by the Netherlands corporation, Akzo, N.V., was the largest rock salt mine in the western hemisphere. In 1994, salt pillars supporting the roof of the mine collapsed allowing water to enter the mine. Large depressions appeared in the ground over portions of the mine, and the mine had to be closed.

The Retsof mine, one thousand feet below the surface, was part of a salt bed that extended from the Province of Ontario to Virginia, and from Michigan to Syracuse. The mine shafts were sunk through Onondaga limestone and dolomite about 500 to 600 feet below the surface, bounded above by four types of shale, Cardif, Skaneateles, Ludlowville, and Marcellus, and below by two types, Camillus and Vernon.

The mine extended for 6,000 acres under three towns; it had over 300 miles of tunnels and passageways. Salt mines are generally safer than other mines; salt is neither flammable nor subject to explosion and is not considered a health hazard. Approximately half of the salt mined by Akzo is rock salt, and the other half is classified as "table salt." In addition to seasoning food, table salt is used in the manufacturing of blue dye and elastic, in oil drilling, and for providing a filler in cosmetics, household cleaners, laundry detergent, and toothpaste.

The mine at Retzof was established by the Empire Salt Company in 1885. It was named by the first president of Empire Salt, William Foster; Retsof is Foster spelled backwards. One of the early shafts was sunk at Cuylerville and was subsequently closed. It was considered to be the haunt of the "blue lady." Many consider the phenomenon of the blue glow to be escaping methane gas; others claim to have see the ghost of a woman carrying a lantern in search of her husband, who lost his life in the mine.

Akzo N. V. bought the Diamond Crystal Salt Company in 1988, merged it with International Salt, and renamed the merged companies Akzo Salt. Akzo Salt is the largest salt company in the world.

153

Syracuse

Father Simon LeMoyne, a French missionary, recorded in his journal of August 16, 1654, that he had found a salt spring near the head of Onondaga Lake. Indians and fur traders took salt from the springs to both Albany and Montreal. The source of the name Onondaga was the Indian word On-on-dah-ka, which meant "swamp at the foot of a hill."

Comfort Tyler settled in the Syracuse area in the late eighteenth century. He cleared the first land, and built the first turnpike road in the region. Tyler was also one of the earliest to become involved in the manufacture of salt. The Onondaga Indians called him To-whan-ta-qua, the man who can do two things at once. James Geddes, another early settler who became involved early in the salt industry, set up his evaporating kettles on the southwest corner of Onondaga Lake.

As the demand for salt grew and the surface brine was used up, wells were sunk 1,200 feet into the salt strata. Beginning in 1821, a solar evaporation method was used to reclaim the salt. In poor weather, the vats were covered with sliding roofs. Eventually, over 10,000 shed structures were built. Salt production peaked in 1862, when nine million bushels of salt were shipped. More readily accessible salt was discovered in the West, and the salt industry in Syracuse waned.

Seneca Lake

The salt industry began on Seneca Lake in 1892 when the Glen Salt Company, later the International Salt Company, first drilled a well on the west shore of the lake, just north of Watkins Glen. Salt is not mined on Seneca Lake; a different process is used to extract the salt from the ground. A well is drilled from 1,800 to 3,000 feet deep to reach a salt deposit, water is pumped down one well to make a brine, the brine is pumped up to the ground level from an adjacent well, and the brine is transported to large evaporators. Water is evaporated off using a heating and cooling process that leaves pure salt in crystalline form, which is virtually table-ready. Only two ingredients are added; one makes the salt free-running, and the other is an iodized solution for iodized salt.

International Salt, now part of the Akzo Salt Company, also makes salt pressed into small small cubes called salt buttons for use in home water softeners, and block salt for livestock.

In 1896, the Watkins Salt Company began operation at the southern end of Seneca Lake, in the village of Watkins Glen. The former Watkins Salt Company is now part of Cargill, Incorporated. The veins of salt under the Seneca Lake region extend northward through New York State into Ontario, Canada.

Cayuga Lake

The salt industry on Cayuga Lake began when the Cayuga Lake Salt Company was formed in 1891. In 1899, the Cayuga Lake Salt Company was consolidated into the National Salt Company, which subsequently was purchased by Cargill, Inc. The company mines salt in the Ludlowville / Myers area, where the veins of salt are 2,000 feet underground.

 ## The Story of the Chemung Canal

he Chemung Canal, which was built between Elmira and Watkins Glen from 1829 to 1833, was officially opened for traffic in October, 1833. A proposal to build the canal had been presented to the New York State Legislature late in the eighteenth century. That proposal to open up the region for commerce was not approved.

However, with the opening of the Erie Canal in 1825, interest in canal transportation was elevated, and the state legislature authorized spending $300,000 to build the Chemung Canal. The actual construction cost was $314,396. Since the canal was built before the availability of the power shovel, the digging was done with pick and shovel. Occasionally, large rocks and trees were blasted out of the way with black powder.

Between Elmira and Watkins Glen, the canal went through Horseheads, Pine Valley, Millport, and Montour Falls, which was called Havana at the time. The canal had forty-nine locks spread over its twenty-three-mile length; its highest elevation was 920 feet at Pine Valley. It was four feet deep, twenty-six feet wide at the bottom, and forty-two feet wide at the surface of the water. Barges

were pulled by horses or mules walking along the towpath. Heavy hemp ropes from the barges were fastened to the animals' harnesses.

A feeder canal was built from Chimney Rocks on the Chemung River at Gibson, just east of Corning, through Big Flats via the Sing Sing Creek to Horseheads. The feeder canal had three locks to accommodate the difference in elevation over its sixteen-mile length. Flood gates at Gibson regulated the supply of water from the Chemung River.

Each canal boat could carry eighty-five to ninety tons of cargo. Less than 20,000 tons were transported in the first year of the canal's operation. Traffic increased over its life until reaching a peak of 270,978 tons in 1854. Traffic began to decline after this point, because many shippers transported their material by railroad. The Erie Railroad completed a line through Elmira in 1849. Manufacturers could ship their coal, flour, lumber, and salt less expensively via rail.

The Story of the Erie Canal

One of the first people to suggest the construction of a canal connecting Lake Erie with the Hudson River was Gouverneur Morris in 1803. In 1810, he was appointed to a commission to plan the canal. James Geddes, a lawyer and surveyor from Syracuse, was employed to survey the prospective route of the canal. On July 4, 1817, construction of the 83-lock Erie Canal along a 364-mile route from Albany to Buffalo began at Rome. The ninety-four-mile section of the canal from Rome west to the Seneca River was constructed first, because it crossed a long, flat stretch of favorable terrain requiring only six locks. Also, it was easier to dig than other sections, and the landowners were more receptive.

Governor DeWitt Clinton sent Canvass White to England to study canal-building techniques. White came home and experimented with various types of cements. He discovered a hydraulic cement that would set under water. It was made from limestone that he burned and mixed with sand. This breakthrough saved considerable time and money in constructing the canal. Built with sloping sides, the canal was forty feet wide at the top and twenty-eight feet wide at the bottom, with a towpath along one side. The water was only four feet deep.

The canal builders constructed eighteen aqueducts to carry the canal over rivers and streams and contended with a difference in elevation of 568 feet between Lake Erie and the Hudson River. Two of the most difficult projects during the construction were digging through rock in the eastern section of the canal near Albany and accommodating a sixty-foot drop in elevation at Lockport. Nathan Roberts solved the problem at Lockport with a double set of five-step locks, one set each for eastbound and westbound traffic.

In 1823, the canal from Rochester to Albany was opened; the cost of shipping a barrel of flour between those two cities dropped from $3.00 to $.75. The full length of the Erie Canal was opened in 1825 with the ceremony-filled Buffalo to Albany cruise of Governor DeWitt Clinton on the *Seneca Chief*. Two barrels of water were transported by the Governor to dump into New York harbor, symbolizing the joining of the two bodies of water. The $7,000,000 spent to build the canal ($2,000,000 over the original estimate) was not considered a sound expenditure by the populace. They were proved wrong. The canal was economically successful beyond even Clinton's dreams.

The use of the canal quickly outstripped its capacity, and traffic jams became commonplace. Between 1835 and 1862, many changes were made in the canal to facilitate the increased traffic: the width at the top of the canal was increased from 40 feet to 70 feet, the width at the bottom was expanded from 28 to 56 feet, and the depth was increased from 4 feet to 7 feet. In addition, the waterway was straightened, the number of locks was reduced from 83 to 72, and at most lock locations a double lock was built to allow two-way traffic.

By the beginning of the twentieth century, railroads provided stiff competition for the Erie Canal. Canal managers wanted to take advantage of advanced engineering skills and steam tugboats. Construction began in 1905 to increase lock sizes to 45 feet wide

by 328 feet long, reduce the number of locks from 72 to 35, and increase the depth of the canal from 7 feet to 12 feet.

Many of the rivers along the route of the canal that were not used during earlier construction were incorporated now, including the Clyde, Oneida, Oswego, Mohawk, and Seneca rivers. The canal system was comprised of the new Erie Canal, the Cayuga-Seneca Canal between Cayuga and Seneca Lakes, the Oswego Canal from Syracuse to Oswego, and the Champlain Canal from Albany to Lake Champlain. It was called the New York State Barge Canal System when it opened in 1918.

The new canal system carried increasing amounts of traffic, but, eventually, efficient railroad freight traffic and truck traffic brought commercial use of the canal to an end. In the late 1950s, the death blow was delivered by the completion of the New York State Thruway and the St. Lawrence Seaway, which linked the Great Lakes with the Atlantic Ocean.

 ## The Story of Esperanza

speranza is an impressive nineteen-room Greek Revival mansion with two-story Ionic columns and 6,000 square feet of space; it overlooks the bluff and the west branch of Keuka Lake from a hillside north of Route 54A and east of Branchport. Construction was completed on July 3, 1838, by its owner, John Nicholas Rose, who purchased over 1,000 acres of land in Yates County in 1823.

The mansion was a wedding gift to his wife, and the name Esperanza was his adaptation of the Latin word for hope. He was the son of Robert Selden Rose and Jane Lawson Rose, who moved from Virginia to the site of the Rose Hill Mansion, near Geneva, in 1804. They brought their slaves with them, but freed them upon completion of their home overlooking the east shore of Seneca Lake.

Esperanza in Jerusalem near Branchport

Two and a half years were spent gathering stone for the cellar walls of Esperanza, which included boulders weighing up to 1,400 pounds. The walls are twenty-seven inches thick, the windows are six feet high, and there are seven fireplaces in the mansion—including one in the basement and two that are plastered over. A large bake-oven hearth in the kitchen is one of the two that are "hidden." Originally, an open staircase extended from the first floor near the entrance to the attic, which is networked with structural beams.

Esperanza is constructed of walls of stone with brick pilasters covered with stucco. Sand for use in mixing the stucco was brought from the tip of Bluff Point, eight miles to the south, in Indian canoes. The weight-bearing interior partitions are solid masonry from the basement to the attic. The Ionic columns on the portico were made by enclosing large tree trunks in brick and then covering the brick with stucco.

The mansion has been the subject of a novel and the location for a movie. It has served as a private residence, a stop on the underground railroad, a sheep barn, the Yates County Home, an art gallery, and Chateau Esperanza winery.

In an interview with Bennett Loudon of the Rochester *Democrat and Chronicle*, Merrill Roenke, the administrator of Rose Hill Mansion near Geneva, observed, "It's a great house ... I think Esperanza is an important building ... They're not building property like this today. It gives you a reflection of the first half of the nineteenth century and the life these people led. If you don't have that, you don't know any of the history of it. They are places of great beauty and we need some beauty in the world." Amen.

The Story of the Genesee Valley Canal

anal construction was a popular activity in the United States during the first half of the nineteenth century. With the completion of the Erie Canal in 1825, residents of the Genesee Valley petitioned for the construction of a canal to connect the Erie Canal with the Allegheny River. The proposed canal would open up markets in Pittsburgh and the Ohio River Valley to western New York merchants. Charles Carroll of Groveland and Micah Brooks of Nunda proposed legislation to authorize the building of the new waterway.

In 1827, Governor DeWitt Clinton proposed "the survey of a route for a canal, to unite the Erie Canal at Rochester with the Allegheny River." James Geddes, the engineer who surveyed the Erie Canal, surveyed a potential route for the canal. The New York State Legislature authorized the construction of the Genesee Valley Canal on May 6, 1836. The proposed canal would extend from Rochester to Olean, with a branch to Dansville. The bed of the canal from Rochester to Sonyea, with the side-cut to Dansville, was relatively flat and few locks were required; this section of the canal opened in 1841.

The canal's route from Nunda south was through rocky, rugged country, particularly in the "Deep Cut" near Oakland. An attempt was made to dig a tunnel over 1,100 feet long, 27 feet wide, and 20 feet high through the palisade below the Middle Falls at Portage. Elisha Johnson, who was to become Rochester's fifth mayor, directed the effort until it was stopped by landslides. The canal route was altered and continued on through Fillmore, Houghton, Caneadea, Belfast, and Cuba. The only sign of Johnson's unsuccessful tunneling attempt is a hole in the cliff wall opposite Letchworth Park's Inspiration Point.

The Genesee Valley Canal was joined with the Allegheny River in 1862. The canal was 125 miles long. It contributed to the success of the Erie Canal by feeding traffic to it, but it was not financially successful itself. With the high cost of canal maintenance and the proliferation of railroads in the last half of the 1800s, the Canal was no longer competitive. It was closed in 1878; the right of way was sold in 1880 to the Genesee Valley Canal Railroad Company, which built a railroad along the towpath of the canal.

The Genesee Valley benefited from the canal. The lumber industry cleared the land and shipped the lumber via the canal. Wheat was cultivated on many of the cleared acres. The lumber was used to build new homes and businesses. The canal was a significant contributing factor to the increase of prosperity in the region.

The Story of the Keuka Outlet Trail

The outlet from Keuka Lake drops about 300 feet in elevation over its six-mile length from Penn Yan to Dresden on Seneca Lake. The outlet, called Minneseta by the Seneca Indians, has the appearance of a trout stream for most of its length. Over its history, the Keuka outlet has been a navigable canal with twenty-seven locks, part of a railroad bed, and the site of over eleven mills and many factories and distilleries.

Among the first settlers to the area were twenty-five members of a religious sect, who arrived in 1788 led by James Parker, a follower of Jemima Wilkinson, an evangelical, non-denominational preacher known as the Publick Universal Friend. The sect, which originated in Rhode Island, moved to the wilderness to get away from the world's temptations. Initially, they chose a site called City Hill near Dresden, one mile south of the outlet stream. They called their settlement Jerusalem or Friend's settlement, after their leader.

In 1790, the town of City Hill had a population of 260 people, which was more than Canandaigua and Geneva combined. The followers of the Publick Universal Friend built the first mill on the Keuka outlet, about halfway between Penn Yan and Dresden. They located it at the highest waterfall (thirty-five feet high), on the future site of Seneca Mills. They purchased their millstones at New Milford, Connecticut, and hauled them upstream from

Dresden on sleds pulled by oxen.

By 1820, there were seven gristmills, one oil mill, fourteen sawmills, and several distilleries along the length of the outlet. Eventually, the outlet became the home of paper mills, plaster mills, potash mills, tanneries, as well as factories producing many products, including chemicals (such as carbon bisulfide), corrugated cardboard, handles, hoops, shingles, wheel spokes, and tools. During the late nineteenth century and the early twentieth century, thirty to forty factories and mills were active at one time.

The Crooked Lake Canal along the outlet went into operation with twelve dams and twenty-seven lift locks in 1833. Because operating expenses consistently exceeded its income, it was abandoned by the state in 1873. However, the outlet survived as a transportation corridor when the Fall Brook Railroad was built in 1884, partly in the canal bed and partly on the towpath. The railroad spurred a new industry along the outlet, the manufacture of paper from straw. Most of the mills had closed by 1930, and the railroad, which had become part of the Penn-Central System, discontinued service in 1972 after being severely damaged in the spring flooding that year.

The railroad right of way was purchased by Yates County in 1981 at the urging of John Sheridan, the Yates County attorney. He suggested using the railroad bed for a hiking trail, which is now called the Keuka Outlet Trail. A memorial to John Sheridan, consisting of a large boulder and a brass plaque, is located adjacent to the trail at the Seneca Millsite, near the the trail's midpoint.

The trail is approximately six feet wide for most of its length and is an excellent hiking trail; it slopes sightly downhill from Penn Yan to Dresden. The trail has eleven millsite markers and is rich with flora and fauna, as well as history. Several of the mills remain, but most of them are noted by a foundation and a marker or just a marker.

The Story of the Mt. Morris Dam

he Mt. Morris Dam, located forty miles south of Rochester near the village of Mt. Morris, extends across a deep gorge of the Genesee River at the northern end of Letchworth State Park. Construction of the dam was authorized by Congress in the Flood Control Act of 1944, and was completed in 1952 by the U.S. Army Corps of Engineers. The concrete gravity dam is 1,028 feet long, 20 feet wide at the top, and 221 feet wide at its base. The top of the dam is 790 feet above sea level and is 215 feet above the streambed.

The spillway is 550 feet long and has a crest elevation of 760 feet. Water is released through nine five-foot by seven-foot con-duits in the base of the spillway sections. The capacity of the reser-voir is 301,600 acre-feet (one acre of water one foot deep). The Flood Control Pool is seventeen river-miles long and 3,300 acres in area.

The dam and reservoir provide flood protection to farms, industrial sites, and residential areas for sixty-seven miles extend-ing to Rochester and the mouth of the Genesee River in Lake Ontario. The facility was built to reduce the threat of floods in the region. A severe flood in 1865 developed water flows in excess of twenty-four million gallons per minute, which is over half the flow of Niagara Falls. A major flood ravaged the Genesee River Valley an average of every seven years from 1865 to 1950.

In the first 32 years of operation, the dam and reservoir pre-vented an estimated $344 million of damage, $210 million of which was estimated to have been prevented during tropical storm "Agnes" in June, 1972. From June 15 to November 1, a conserva-tion pool elevation of 600 feet is maintained to enhance the scenic beauty of Letchworth State Park.

The Story of the Rochester Subway

n 1921, two years after the last barge passed through Rochester on the Erie Canal, the City of Rochester purchased from the state the canal right-of-way through the city and through the towns of Brighton, Greece, and Pittsford. In November, 1921, Mayor Edgerton signed the ordinance that authorized the construction of the Rochester subway. Construction was authorized to provide an interconnecting "belt line" for freight traffic for the five steam railroads serving the city and to remove the interurban electric trolley cars from the downtown streets

From the time of the opening of the Erie Canal in 1825, many of Rochester's industries had located along the waterway. The proposed subway was considered to be an inexpensive way to provide freight service to those businesses. Its route facilitated interconnections with the five steam railroads and the Barge Canal terminal near Mt. Hope Avenue on the east bank of the Genesee River. It was predicted that 20,000 freight cars a year would use the subway.

Four interurban railways had begun serving Rochester between 1900 and 1910: the Rochester & Eastern Rapid Railway, the Rochester, Lockport & Buffalo Railway, the Rochester & Sodus Bay Railway, and the Rochester & Syracuse Railway. The interurban cars were larger than city trolley cars and occasionally were operated as trains. They operated on the existing trolley car tracks and, because of their size, put pedestrians and other vehicles at risk. Also, the interurban cars traveled at faster speeds than street railways and frequently derailed on sharp curves designed for slower speeds.

In 1912, nineteen fatal traffic accidents occurred in downtown Rochester. Main Street, on which many of the accidents occurred, was called the "Aisle of Death." Pressure to remove the interurban cars from city streets grew as the accident statistics increased. Other advantages of building the subway were the addition of a roof over the canal downtown and the construction of an upper deck on the canal aqueduct over the Genesee River. Traffic congestion downtown would be reduced considerably by the addition of a roadway (Broad Street) parallel to Main Street.

In 1920, City Engineer E. A. Fisher initiated plans to use the abandoned Erie Canal bed for an industrial and interurban railway. His plan included three parts:

- Constructing the covered portion from South Avenue to Brown Street
- Widening and deepening the canal bed and building new bridges at intersecting streets
- Constructing of the overhead electrical system, interchanges, sidings, a signal system, stations, and tracks

Work began on the subway in May, 1922. The canal bed from the Genesee aqueduct to Oak Street was dug sufficiently wide to accommodate four sets of tracks, and an overhead clearance of seventeen feet was provided.

Tracks for most of the rest of the subway were laid in an open cut. This included the section from South Avenue to the eastern terminus and from Oak Street to the western terminus. The canal bed also was widened and deepened in these sections to accommodate up to four sets of tracks. Three subway stations were built downtown: Court Street station at South Avenue, City Hall station between Exchange and Fitzhugh streets, and the station at West Main and Oak streets.

The subway was completed in late 1927 at a cost of $12,000,000. Barely three years after it was completed, the interurban electric railways, with which it was connected, began to fail. On July 31, 1930, the Rochester & Eastern Rapid Railway went out of business due to competition from increased motor vehicle traffic to Pittsford and Canandaigua. In April of the following year, the Rochester, Lockport & Buffalo switched to buses, and, two months later, the Rochester & Syracuse ceased operation. This left the Rochester & Sodus Bay, renamed the Rochester Transit Company, to operate the nine-mile-long subway using cars from the old Sodus Bay line. Fortunately, use of the freight transfer facilities that supported the five steam railroads increased.

The subway generated deficits every year, which caused Rochester Transit to increase the fares on the surface lines to make up the difference. The local trolley service, a subsidiary of New

York State Railways, operated under the threat of foreclosure against the state-owned parent after 1929. Since the Rochester trolley lines operated at a profit, the city considered buying the lines; however, the 1930 valuation of $26,695,000 exceeded the city's borrowing capacity.

During the 1930s, the City of Rochester's credit was burdened by welfare debts due to the Depression. By 1938, when the Public Service Commission approved the purchase of the trolley lines by private investors, buses had become the preferred method of travel. The new privately-owned company replaced the trolleys with buses, and, by early 1940, trolleys had disappeared from all lines except the subway.

After being considered a white elephant for most of its life, the subway experienced a boom during the early 1940s. Gas rationing and the shortage of automobiles during World War II doubled the number of passengers carried by the subway. In 1947, it transported over 5,000,000 passengers.

City Commerce Commissioner Harold McFarlin was so optimistic that he recommended extending the subway northward to Kodak Park and southward to a more accessible suburban terminal. However, a significant drop in the subway's ridership in 1948 forestalled the suggested expansion. Two consultants evaluated the economics of operating the subway; they recommended dropping the passenger service and concentrating on the freight service.

The resumption of the production of automobiles after World War II, and the public's love affair with cars sounded the death knell for the subway. The construction of the New York State Thruway in the late 1940s and early 1950s, with connections at LeRoy, Route 15, and Victor, also contributed to its demise. The subway operated at a loss of $48,929 in 1950, and its projected loss for 1951 was $56, 000.

In 1951, the subway was shut down. It could no longer compete with buses, cars, and trucks. The subway apppeared to be a good idea when it was conceived, but, with the exception of the World War II years, it struggled financially for most of its life. Part of the subway right-of-way along the Erie Canal bed is now an expressway (Route 490). For many Rochester residents, the topic of the subway is still a nostalgia trip.

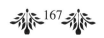

The Story of the Smith Opera House

The Smith Opera House, 82 Seneca Street, Geneva, is both a movie theatre and a theatre for the performing arts. Its forty-two- by thirty-foot movie screen is the largest in central New York. The opera house is one of only twenty-one "Great American Movie Palaces" left in New York, of which only five are still used as performing arts facilities. One of the five is Radio City Music Hall in New York City. Only 304 of the more than 3,000 theatres of this type built in the United States still exist. The Smith Opera House was almost destroyed in 1981 to provide space for a parking lot, but was saved by the Finger Lakes Regional Arts Council.

Due to the modifications that it underwent over the years, its architecture is an eclectic mixture of Art-Deco, Spanish-Baroque, and Victorian styles. The theatre's original facade was "Richardsonian," with a terra cotta arch carved with the likenesses of Edwin Booth and William Shakespeare. The walls on the sides of the stage have golden cartouches with busts of Beethoven and Moliere. The theatre has excellent acoustics, and an unobstructed view of the stage is provided from all 1,400 seats.

Geneva philanthropist William Smith paid $39,000 in 1894 to fulfill his dream of an opera house for the city. It opened on October 29, 1894, with James O'Neill, the father of playwright Eugene O'Neill, starring in the play "The Count of Monte Cristo." Other famous entertainers who have performed at the opera house are Sarah Bernhardt, George M. Cohan, Tommy Dorsey, Isadora Duncan, Arthur Fiedler, Al Jolson, John Philip Sousa, and Ellen Terry.

The Smith Opera House was used as a vaudeville house / playhouse until the early 1900s, when it was donated to Hobart College. Hobart sold it to help endow William Smith College at its founding in 1908. Schine Enterprises bought the building in 1929, and totally renovated it to be the flagship of the Schine chain of theatres. Architect Victor Rigaumount designed a ceiling of stars in an evening sky, utilized Art Deco style signs and trim, and chose Victorian-style light fixtures.

Performances at the Smith Opera House in recent years have included the Acrobats from the Peoples' Republic of China, the Berkshire Ballet's Nutcracker, the Rochester Philharmonic Orchestra, Bruce Springsteen, the Syracuse Symphony Orchestra conducted by Mitch Miller, and the U.S. Air Force Band of the East. The Smith Opera House is the home of the Finger Lakes Symphony Orchestra and the Geneva Theatre Guild.

 **The Story of the Willard Memorial Chapel**

he Willard Memorial Chapel, at 17 Nelson Street, Auburn, was built for the Auburn Theological Seminary in 1892-94, as a memorial to Dr. Sylvester D. Willard and his wife, Jane Frances Case, from their daughters. At the time the chapel was being constructed, the seminary received a bequest from former professor R. B. Welch for the construction of a new classroom building. All that remains today of the Auburn Theological Seminary is the Willard Memorial Chapel and the adjoining Welch Memorial Building, with over 8,000 feet of usable space.

The two Romanesque Revival buildings are built of gray Cayuga County limestone trimmed with red portage stone and are joined by an enclosed walkway. The architect was A. J. Warner of Rochester, and the builder was Barnes and Stout of Auburn. Both buildings are on the New York Register of Historic Places and the National Register of Historic Places. The Auburn Theological Seminary closed it doors in 1939 and became part of the Union Theological Seminary in New York City.

The Willard Memorial Chapel, which seats 250, is unique in having been designed by Louis Comfort Tiffany. Many buildings and museums have a Tiffany lamp, plaque, or window, but the entire interior of the Willard Memorial Chapel was designed by Tiffany, including the ceiling, chairs, chandeliers, floors, glass mosaics, pews, walls, windows, and the memorial plaque. Harold Jaffe, president of the Louis Comfort Tiffany Society, calls the

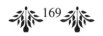

chapel "the only complete religious building extant in the United States designed by Louis Comfort Tiffany."

A gilt bronze and mosaic glass memorial tablet dominates the wall to the left of the entrance. It is an 18-foot by 9-foot bas-relief of a angel with extended wings, looking upward toward the memorial inscription to Dr. and Mrs. Willard. St. John the Baptist and the Holy Spirit are on one side of the angel, and Hope and Charity are on the other. The angel is holding a scroll with the inscription, "And now bideth Faith, Hope, and Love, these three, but the greatest of these is Love." The memorial plaque is surrounded by a border of Tiffany mosaic.

The largest Tiffany "Favrile" glass window in the chapel, directly above the memorial plaque, displays Christ sustaining St. Peter on the waves of Lake Genesareth. Tiffany derived the name "Favrile" from the Anglo-Saxon word for "handmade." Nine "Mooresque" style chandeliers designed by Tiffany hang from the vaulted wood ceiling. They are made of jeweled and leaded glass with crystal pendants hanging from them and are mounted in bronze.

A row of seven oak chairs, inlaid with glass and metal mosaic, is placed behind the carved oak / gold stenciled pulpit. Singing in the chapel was accompanied by a large Steere and Turner tracker organ. Other features of the chapel include fourteen opalescent windows, mosaic floors, and oak wainscoting.

One well-known family associated with the Auburn Theological Seminary was the Dulles family. Reverend Allen Macy Dulles moved to Auburn with his family in 1904 to teach at the seminary and to serve as pastor of the Second Presbyterian Church. One of Reverend Dulles' sons, John Foster Dulles, served as Secretary of State and another son, Allen Welch Dulles, was the Director of the Central Intelligence Agency.

The interior of the chapel was almost auctioned off in the late 1980s, but was saved by the Community Preservation Committee of Auburn. The Seventh-Day Adventist Church, owners of the chapel from 1957 until 1988, decided to build a new church that would be more economical to heat. The chapel was sold to an antique dealer, who planned to dismantle and sell the interior. However, the preservation committee prevailed upon him to sell the chapel to them for $500,000 (even though individual Tiffany lamps sold for $480,000 in 1987).

The Community Preservation Committee plans to continue the chapel's use as a place of interfaith worship and a setting for functions such as concerts and weddings. Tours are conducted that focus on the chapel's art, architecture, and history.

Epilogue Poem

Ye say they all have passed away,
    That noble race and brave,
That their light canoes have vanished
    From off the crested wave;
That 'mid the forest where they roamed
    There rings no hunters' shout;

But their name is on your waters,
    Ye may not wash it out.
Ye say their cone-like cabins
    That clustered o'er the vale,
Have fled like withered leaves
    Before the Autumn's gale;
But their memory liveth on your hills,
    Their baptism on your shore;
Your everlasting rivers speak
    Their dialect of yore.

From "Indian Names" by Lydia Huntley Sigourney

Bibliography

Abbott, C. G. *The 1914 Tests of the Langley "Aerodrome."* Washington, D.C.: Smithsonian Institution, 1942.

Ackerman, Carl W. *George Eastman.* Boston: Houghton Mifflin, 1930.

Amberger, Ron, Dick Barrett, and Greg Marling. *Canal Boats, Interurbans, & Trolleys.* Rochester, N.Y.: National Railway Historical Society, 1985.

Balio, Tino, ed. *The American Film Industry.* Madison: U of Wisconsin P, 1976.

Beach, S. A. *The Apples of New York*, Vol.1. Albany: J. B. Lyon, 1905.

Beauchamp, William M. *Iroquois Folk Lore.* Port Washington, N. Y.: Ira J. Friedman, 1965.

Boller, Paul F., Jr. *Presidential Anecdotes.* New York: Oxford UP, 1981.

Bonner, Frederick Lidell, George Frederick Howe, and Hiram C. Todd. *Chester Alan Arthur, Class of 1848.* Schenectady: Union College Press, 1948.

Brown, Francis. *Raymond of the Times.* New York: Norton, 1951.

Bruchac, Joseph. *Iroquois Stories: Heroes and Heroines Monsters and Magic.* Trumansburg, N. Y.: Crossing Press, 1985.

Canfield, William W. *The Legends of the Iroquois.* Port Washington, N.Y.: Ira J. Friedman, 1971.

Carmer, Carl. *Dark Trees to the Wind: A Cycle of York State Years.* New York: W.S. Lowe Associates, 1949.

---. *Listen for a Lonesome Drum: A New York State Chronicle.* New York: Farrar & Rinehart, 1936.

The Chronicle-Express. Penn Yan, N. Y., "Summer Issue," various.

Converse, Harriet Maxwell. *Myths and Legends of the New York State Iroquois*. Albany: SUNY, 1908

Cornplanter, Jesse J. *Legends of the Longhouse*. Port Washington, N. Y.: Ira J. Friedman, 1963.

Cramer, C. H. *Royal Bob: The Life of Robert G. Ingersoll*. Indianapolis: Bobbs-Merrill, 1952.

Davis, Miles A. *The History of Jerusalem*. N.p.: n.p., 1912.

Harris, Sherwood. *The First to Fly: Aviation's Pioneer Days*. Blue Ridge Summit, PA: Tab Aero, 1970.

Heidt, William, Jr. *0-WE-NAH: A Legend of Lake Eldridge*. Ithaca: DeWitt Society of Tompkins County, 1971.

Hinman, A. P. *How a British Subject Became President of the United States*. New York: n.p., 1884.

Howe, George Frederick. *Chester A. Arthur: A Quarter-Century of Machine Politics*. New York: Frederick Ungar, 1935.

Hubbard, J. Niles. *An Account of Sa-Go-Ye-Wat-Ha or Red Jacket and His People*. New York: Burt Franklin, 1886.

Huggins, Nathan Irwin. *Slave and Citizen: The Life of Frederick Douglass*. Boston: Little, Brown, 1980.

Josephy, Alvin M., Jr. *The Indian Heritage of America*. Boston: Houghton Mifflin, 1968.

Klees, Emerson. *People of the Finger Lakes Region*. Rochester, N. Y.: Friends of the Finger Lakes Publishing, 1995.

---. *Persons, Places, and Things Around The Finger Lakes Region*. Rochester, N. Y.: Friends of the Finger Lakes Publishing, 1994.

---. *Persons, Places, and Things In the Finger Lakes Region*. Rochester, N. Y.: Friends of the Finger Lakes Publishing, 1993.

Loudon, Bennett J. "Historic Home's New Lease on Life." Rochester *Democrat and Chronicle*. 27 Aug. 1995: 3B.

McKelvey, Blake. *Rochester: An Emerging Metropolis 1925-1961*. Rochester, N.Y.: Christopher Press, 1961.

---. *Rochester: The Quest for Quality 1890-1925*. Cambridge: Harvard UP, 1956.

Merrill, Arch. *Bloomers and Bugles*. New York: American Book-Stratford, 1958.

---. *Fame in Our Time.* New York: American Book-Stratford, 1960.

---. *From Pumpkin Hook to Dumpling Hill.* New York: American Book-Stratford, 1969.

---. *Gaslights and Gingerbread.* New York: American Book-Stratford, 1959.

---. *Shadows on the Wall.* New York: American Book-Stratford. n.d.

---. *Southern Tier, Vol. 2.* New York: American Book-Stratford, 1954.

---. *Tomahawks and Old Lace.* Rochester, N. Y.: Democrat and Chronicle, 1948.

---. *The Towpath.* Rochester, N. Y.: Democrat and Chronicle, 1945.

---. *The White Woman and Her Valley.* New York: American Book-Stratford, n.d.

New York State Department of Agriculture & Markets. *New York State Apple Facts from the "Apple Country."* Albany: n.p., 1972.

Onondaga Historical Association. "The Franklin: Syracuse's Automotive Heritage." 3 (1992)

Parker, Arthur C. *Seneca Myths and Folk Tales.* Buffalo: Buffalo Historical Society, 1923.

Smith, Erminnie A. *Myths of the Iroquois.* Washington, D. C.: Smithsonian Institution, 1883.

Skinner, Charles M. *American Myths and Legends.* Philadelphia: Lippincott, 1974.

Schmidt, Carl F. *Cobblestone Architecture.* Rochester, N.Y.: n.p., 1944.

Stinson, Donald J. *The Burning of the Frontenac.* Interlaken, N.Y.: Heart of the Lakes Publishing, 1985.

Taylor, Eva. *A Short History of Elmira.* Elmira: Steele Memorial Library, 1937.

Taylor, John. "The Painter and the President." *Civil War Times Illustrated.* Jan. / Feb. 1992: 21-26.

Thompson, Stith., ed. *Tales of the North American Indians.* Bloomington: Indiana UP, 1929.

Wade, Garth. "Return of a Fine Winery." *New York State's Southern Tier Shopper: 1995 Vacation Guide.* Hammondsport, N.Y.: Gwen Lee Associates, 1995.

Williamson, Samuel T. *Imprint of a Publisher: The Story of Frank Gannett and His Independent Newspapers.* Toronto: Robert M. McBride, 1948.

Wolfson, Evelyn. *The Iroquois: People of the Northeast.* Brookfield, Connecticut: Millbrook Press, 1992.

List of Illustrations   Page No.